"Okay, we've got a malfunction,"
David said, just a little nervously.

Wishbone watched the control room carefully. He saw David and the shuttle mission commander begin to look through their lists of malfunction solutions.

Come on, come on, come on! Fix the problem, Wishbone thought. *Lives are at stake here!*

Then Wishbone saw a second malfunction light. David was so busy studying his manual, he didn't notice this one. Neither did anyone else.

Wishbone turned to David. "Flight director, this is MWD, Mission Watchdog. I'm afraid we've got another problem."

David didn't seem to hear.

"Flight director," Wishbone said more loudly to David. "I repeat—we are showing a *second* problem." *Why is it no one ever listens to the dog? Not even during a state of emergency!*

Books in The SUPER Adventures of WISHBONE™ series:

Books in The Adventures of WISHBONE™ series:

*coming soon

The SUPER Adventures of WISHBONE

UNLEASHED IN SPACE

by Alexander Steele
Inspired by *The Legion of Space*
by Jack Williamson
WISHBONE™ created by Rick Duffield

Big Red Chair Books™ *A Division of Lyrick Publishing*™

This book is a work of fiction. The characters, incidents, and dialogues are products of the author's imagination and are not to be construed as real. Any resemblance to actual events or persons, living or dead, is entirely coincidental.

 Big Red Chair Books™, *A Division of Lyrick Publishing*™
300 E. Bethany Drive, Allen, Texas 75002

©1999 Big Feats! Entertainment

Edited by Kevin Ryan

Copy edited by Jonathon Brodman

Continuity editing by Grace Gantt

Cover design and interior illustrations by Lyle Miller

Wishbone photograph by Carol Kaelson

Library of Congress Catalog Card Number: 98-89333

ISBN: 1-57064-329-6

First printing: May 1999

10 9 8 7 6 5 4 3 2 1

Printed in the United States of America

*To Jack Williamson,
for allowing Wishbone and me to join
the Legion of Space*

*To the folks at Space Camp in Huntsville, Alabama,
for allowing me to spend a week as
an astronaut-scientist-engineer*

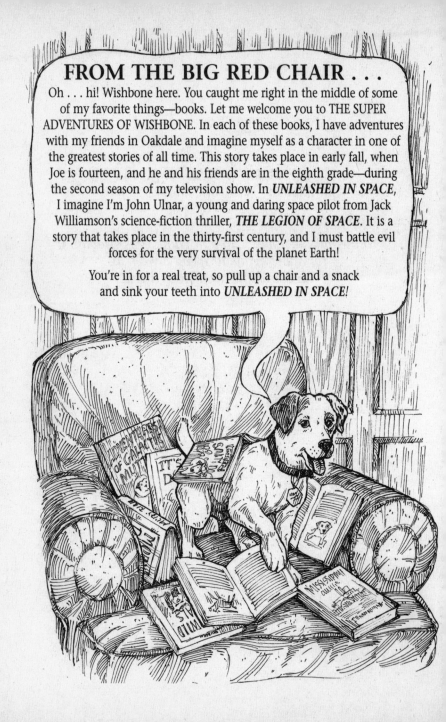

FROM THE BIG RED CHAIR . . .

Oh . . . hi! Wishbone here. You caught me right in the middle of some of my favorite things—books. Let me welcome you to THE SUPER ADVENTURES OF WISHBONE. In each of these books, I have adventures with my friends in Oakdale and imagine myself as a character in one of the greatest stories of all time. This story takes place in early fall, when Joe is fourteen, and he and his friends are in the eighth grade—during the second season of my television show. In *UNLEASHED IN SPACE*, I imagine I'm John Ulnar, a young and daring space pilot from Jack Williamson's science-fiction thriller, *THE LEGION OF SPACE*. It is a story that takes place in the thirty-first century, and I must battle evil forces for the very survival of the planet Earth!

You're in for a real treat, so pull up a chair and a snack and sink your teeth into *UNLEASHED IN SPACE!*

CHAPTER ONE

Wishbone tilted his head upward, admiring a rocket that stood as high as a sixteen-story building. Its narrow white shape looked stunning against the blue autumn sky.

Boy, the places I could go in that thing, the white-with-brown-and-black-spots Jack Russell terrier thought.

Wishbone looked around, seeing about a dozen more rockets of different sizes. The rockets surrounding him were part of Rocket Park, which was on the grounds of the U.S. Space & Rocket Center, in Huntsville, Alabama. Wishbone had learned that the Space & Rocket Center was like a mini-city, containing outdoor exhibits, an indoor museum, an amusement park, and, best of all—Space Camp.

Space Camp was a place where people went to do some real in-depth learning about the many aspects of space travel. There were several different levels of training programs. Space Camp was for grades four through six; Space Academy was for grades seven and eight; Advanced Space Academy was for grades nine through twelve; and there was another version of Space Academy for adults.

7

Wishbone was incredibly excited because he was about to become the first dog to participate in any of the Space Camp programs. He would be attending Space Academy with his three best friends—Joe, Sam, and David—who were all in eighth grade.

"This place is amazing," said Joe Talbot, shielding the afternoon sun away from his face with his hand. Joe was a good-natured fourteen-year-old boy. His chief markings were straight brown hair, an athletic build, and a great smile. He was every bit as good at playing basketball as Wishbone was at stick-chasing. Wishbone lived with Joe in their comfortable house back in the town of Oakdale.

"It's the perfect deal," said Sam Kepler, spreading her arms with pleasure. "Fun enough so it seems like a vacation, but educational enough so our school principal lets us out for it."

Sam's real name was Samantha, but she preferred to go by the nickname "Sam." She attended Sequoyah Middle School with Joe and David. Her chief markings were silky blond hair and hazel eyes. When it came to doing anything that was artistic, Sam was top dog.

David Barnes knelt down to check out a cone-shaped rocket engine. "This is about as close as we can get to the space program without actually working for NASA."

David's chief markings were dark, curly hair and eyes that examined everything with great curiosity. Back in Oakdale, he lived right next door to Joe and Wishbone. David knew about things electrical, mechanical, or generally scientific the way Wishbone knew about bones.

Joe, Sam, and David all had duffel bags with them. Along with a group of other kids, Wishbone and his friends had just been picked up at a nearby airport by a Space Camp counselor.

Wishbone's path to Space Camp had been a very interesting one. A few months earlier, Space Camp had announced an unusual contest. It was designed to honor Laika, a Russian dog that was the first Earth creature sent into space. Boys and girls in the seventh and eighth grades across the country were invited to write an essay about why they should be allowed to attend Space Camp with their pet dog. The winner and his or her dog would receive six free days at Space Academy. Amazingly, Joe had won the contest.

Wishbone knew Joe's essay by heart, having heard Joe read it to a number of people around town. It began:

> Most dogs love adventure, but my dog, Wishbone, has an appetite for adventure that is out of this world. If ever there was a dog destined to reach the stars, it would be Wishbone. . . .

I couldn't have written that better myself, Wishbone thought.

When Sam and David had learned Joe and Wishbone would be attending Space Academy, they knew they had to go along. Sam and David worked tirelessly to raise the money for their expenses. They collected refundable bottles and cans, sold baked goods, did cleaning, yard work, tutoring, and other odd jobs.

Wishbone looked up proudly at his three best friends. "Joe, Sam, David, if I may say something, I believe the next six days are going to be one of the greatest adventures of our lives. And I couldn't be more pleased to share them with the three of you."

The kids looked around at the rockets, as if they hadn't heard Wishbone's words.

Why is it no one listens to the dog? Wishbone wondered. *Huh? Why is that? I say all these amazing things, but sometimes they just don't listen!*

Wishbone followed his friends across the nicely landscaped grounds of the Space & Rocket Center. Soon they came to a building made of giant silver tubes that was designed to look like a space station. This was the Habitat, where the campers would live for the next few days. The group went inside the Habitat, finding the interior just as futuristic-looking as the outside.

A counselor was seated at a table, wearing a dark blue jumpsuit, the Space Camp counselor uniform. A group of youngsters waited in line as the counselor registered them, one at a time. Each kid was given a team assignment, a room assignment, bedding supplies,

towels, a Space Academy T-shirt, a logbook full of information, and an I.D. tag, which the kids were told to wear at all times.

Wishbone was surprised that he wasn't given any of these things, but he decided now was not the time to complain.

4:00 P.M. After dropping their stuff in their dorm rooms, Wishbone and his friends were guided to a high-tech auditorium right near the Habitat. As the kids entered, they were told to sit on separate sides of the room, depending upon which team they had been assigned to.

Joe, Sam, and David sat in chairs, and Wishbone parked himself on the floor of an aisle. They had all been assigned to the Charger team, so named because it was being sponsored by the Charger athletic-drink company.

Soon, lots of other kids were in the room, some talking a mile a minute, others keeping shyly quiet. A quick count told Wishbone that there were two teams, each with sixteen kids. Wishbone noticed a few kids stealing glances at him.

"Sorry, folks," Wishbone announced, "no autographs right now, please."

The kids seemed to understand, because no one approached the dog for an autograph.

A counselor stood up in front of Wishbone's team, an African-American woman in her twenties. She had a sweet, easy way about her, but Wishbone could also tell she was no pushover.

"Hi, there," the counselor greeted the Charger team. "My name is Monique. I'm your night counselor. I will be with you every day from three in the afternoon until eleven at night. Tomorrow you will meet your day counselor, who will be with you every day from seven in the morning until I go on duty. And for the rest of this week, you won't be kids anymore. You'll be 'trainees.'"

"Got it," Wishbone said with a nod.

"Normally, there are a lot more trainees at Space Camp," Monique explained. "But since it's near the start of the school year, we have a smaller group. Just two Academy teams. In the summer, there are hundreds of people around. This is good, though, because things won't be quite so crazy."

Then one of the camp directors appeared at a podium and gave an orientation speech. Among other things, the director introduced Wishbone and explained why the dog was present. He pointed out that a dog had been in space before, and it could happen again. In that spirit, Wishbone should be thought of as a fellow trainee, rather than just a cute canine.

"You bet I'm a trainee," Wishbone whispered to Joe. "And my next stop after camp is outer space!"

5:00 P.M. When the orientation session ended, the Charger team walked with Monique along an outdoor sidewalk. Soon they came to a large, official-looking building. This was the Space Camp Training Center. A sign at the entrance announced: THROUGH THESE DOORS ENTER AMERICA'S FUTURE ASTRONAUTS, SCIENTISTS, AND ENGINEERS.

They ought to put something about astrodogs on that sign, Wishbone thought, as he entered the building. *We can fix that later.*

As Wishbone was learning, everything at Space Academy was done according to a strict schedule. Now it was time for one of the academy's most important activities—dinner. Monique led the Charger team into a cafeteria. Before Joe went through the food line, he made sure Wishbone's dinner was properly laid out. The Space Camp staff had thoughtfully provided Wishbone with a food bowl, water bowl, and his favorite brand of dog food. Wishbone couldn't help but notice the bowls were labeled with the letters "NASA."

Wishbone knew that "NASA" stood for "National Aeronautics and Space Administration." Founded in 1958, it was the government agency that was in charge of the entire United States space program. One of the reasons Space Camp had so much cool stuff was because the camp worked closely with NASA.

Wishbone wasted no time going to work on his dinner. *When I'm done here, I wouldn't mind sampling some of those heavenly smelling hamburgers!*

5:30 P.M. Dinner done, Monique led the Charger team through a hallway of the Training Center, bringing them to the training floor. Just the sight of the place made Wishbone's pink tongue pant with awe.

Beyond a blue railing lay a vast open space about the size of a football field. Arranged around the space were all sorts of high-tech gizmos and a bunch of giant white "vehicles" that looked a lot like spaceships. Along one wall, a collection of glassed-in offices looked down on the training floor from a second floor. On another wall hung a gigantic flag of the United States.

Yessiree. This is some fancy playground . . . uh . . . I mean training ground.

Monique led her team through the railing, down a few steps, and across the polished floor. She had the trainees sit on benches, right near a device that looked like a mechanical swing. A seat hung from the high ceiling by a metal cord that had springs attached.

Monique spoke to the team, her voice sounding very professional. "One of the things you trainees will be doing this week is trying out simulators. Remember, these are not amusement park rides. These are training devices, just like the ones used by real astronauts."

"Got it," Wishbone said with a nod.

"The simulator you're looking at is called the 'one-sixth chair,'" Monique continued. "This chair will let you feel what it would be like to walk on the moon's surface. It's called the one-sixth chair because the moon has only one-sixth of Earth's gravity. As a result, you'll feel as if you weigh only one-sixth of your normal weight."

Monique called up the trainees in reverse alphabetical order. Joe Talbot was first. After Joe put on a helmet, Monique strapped him into the chair. Monique instructed Joe to hop along a red line that was painted on the floor. Then Monique pushed a button, which caused a whirring noise.

Joe hopped up . . . and went up and up until he was six feet off the ground. "Wow!" Joe exclaimed, as he landed lightly on his feet. "I could sure use this thing on the basketball court!"

As everyone watched, Joe hopped along the red line, each hop taking him high off the ground. On his way back down, Joe was instructed by Monique to use a side-to-side movement. On the way up again, Joe was told to use a jogging motion. With every motion, Joe went sailing wondrously far off the floor.

On the way back, Monique told Joe to use any type of movement he desired. Joe jogged forward, his legs covering the floor in big, long bounds. All the way, he was pretending that he was dribbling a basketball. When Joe came to the end of the line, he flew almost ten feet upward, pretending to shoot a layup shot.

As Joe landed, he wore an ear-to-ear grin. "Thanks to NASA, I felt like I was in the NBA. That was awesome!"

One by one, the other trainees tried out the one-sixth chair. Most of them enjoyed it every bit as much as Joe had. Once all the humans had had their turn, Wishbone jumped off his bench and headed for the chair. Monique smiled at the dog, while most of the trainees roared with laughter.

"Monique," Wishbone said eagerly, "send me to the moon!"

Monique quieted the group, then turned to Joe. "I don't see any harm in having Wishbone try the chair. It's up to you, though. He might get frightened."

Joe waved a hand. "Monique, you don't know Wishbone yet. He'll try anything."

Monique pulled the chair down as low as it would go. Then she gently lifted the dog, got him adjusted on the chair, and strapped him in.

Wishbone hung in the air, his paws barely touching the floor. He felt light, springy, as if he weighed only a fraction of his true weight. He took a cautious step . . . and bounced a good twelve inches off the ground.

Okay, I think I'm getting the hang of this.

Growing bolder, Wishbone tried a trot. It was a weird feeling. It seemed as if he was moving in slow motion, but the dog noticed he was traveling great distances along the red line. Every time he came down, Wishbone barely felt any pressure on his paws.

Finally, Wishbone tried a leap. Up—up—up he soared, flying high into the air, as if he were an Olympic athlete.

"Hey, look at me!" Wishbone cried, as he took a few more leaps.

The other trainees were laughing and cheering Wishbone every leap of the way. When Wishbone reached the end of the red line, the counselor went over to him.

"I can see why you were picked for Space Academy," Monique said, as she unstrapped the dog. "Nice work, Wishbone!"

6:30 P.M. It was twilight by the time Wishbone and his fellow team members went back outside. The group walked past Rocket Park and came to a festively lit amusement park. The area contained a variety of space-themed rides that were open to the general public.

The team headed toward a very tall tower that was outlined with bright orange lights. This was a ride called Space Shot. There was a little free time, and some of the trainees had persuaded Monique to let them try the ride.

"This girl was telling me about Space Shot," Sam told Joe and David. "It shoots you up about a hundred and fifty feet. And it does it so fast, you turn weightless for a few seconds."

"Can't wait," Joe said, clapping his hands together. "But I think Wishbone better sit this one out."

"I'll wait down here with Wishbone," David said with a worried look.

Wishbone glanced up at David, remembering that the boy had a slight fear of heights. *An astronaut who doesn't like heights . . . Uh-oh, that doesn't sound too good. It's a bit like a dog who doesn't care about food.*

Wishbone watched Joe, Sam, and ten others climb into seat compartments that went all the way around the base of the Space Shot tower. Safety devices came down over the shoulders of the passengers, securing them in place. Suddenly, Space Shot let loose with a noise that sounded like a tremendous whoosh of wind.

Wishbone heard gleeful screams as he saw his friends shoot straight up at an incredible speed. It seemed as if they might fly all the way out of Earth's atmosphere.

Whoa, that looks exciting! And you know what? This whole thing is reminding me of one of my favorite stories. A space-travel story, of course. It's a science fiction tale that was written in 1934 by Jack Williamson. Science fiction, also known as sci-fi, is a type of story that blends elements of science and fantasy. And sci-fi stories are usually set in the future, like this one.

Okay, prepare for blastoff. Soon we'll be traveling faster than the speed of light and visiting a distant world where dangerous aliens float beneath a reddish sky. We're rocketing into that fantastic tale, *The Legion of Space!*

CHAPTER TWO

Wishbone zoomed through his imagination. He pictured himself as John Ulnar, a young and daring space pilot who lived in the faraway future. The year was 3001, and John Ulnar was about to be swept into one of the most heroic adventures in the history of mankind.

John Ulnar stood firmly on all four legs and raised his ears to attention. "Major Stell, I am reporting for my orders."

John spoke the words with pride. He was about to receive his first orders as a soldier of the Legion of Space. Only yesterday, the twenty-one-year-old John had graduated from the Legion Academy, a training school for Legion officers. The Legion of Space was a military organization whose job it was to protect the Green Government, which ruled Earth and all its colonies throughout the Solar System.

John caught a glimpse of himself in the reflection

of the major's polished desk. He thought he looked quite fit and handsome in his sky-blue jumpsuit, the standard uniform for junior officers. His black belt shone as brightly as his little black nose.

Major Stell looked down at John. He wore the navy-blue jumpsuit of a senior officer of the Legion. The stiff hairs of his crewcut were raised as high as John's ears.

"By any chance," the major said, "are you related to Adam Ulnar?"

"Yes, sir," John replied.

Adam Ulnar was the Supreme Commander of the Legion of Space. As such, he was one of the most powerful persons in the Earth's Solar System—or the "System," as it was commonly known. Adam was a distant relative of John's, and he had arranged for John to be accepted into the Legion Academy. This had surprised John, because the two had met face to face only one time, when John was just a young boy.

The major studied John. "I suppose Supreme Commander Ulnar is the one responsible for getting you this assignment. Normally, this duty is given only to experienced members of the Legion."

John raised his ears even higher, hoping to appear worthy of the assignment. "What is the assignment, sir?"

The major folded his hands on the desk with great seriousness. "This is a mission involving AKKA."

"AKKA?" John said, puzzled. "I've never heard of such a thing."

"It is an abbreviation . . . or symbol . . . or something of the sort."

"Well, whatever it is, sir, I've never heard of it."

"That is because AKKA stands at the highest level of top-secret information."

"I see, but what exactly—"

"More than a few men have died attempting to learn the secret of AKKA."

"I don't wish to die, but what—"

"In short," the major stated, "AKKA is the most precious thing that mankind possesses."

John felt he would jump out of his fur with impatience. "I understand, sir. *But what is it?*"

The major shrugged. "I don't know."

"Oh," John said, his whiskers twitching with confusion.

"Only a handful of people have a general idea of what AKKA is," the major explained. "And only one person knows the exact nature of AKKA. This person is the Keeper of AKKA. The single most important duty of the Legion is to protect this Keeper. You, Lieutenant Ulnar, will be part of a guard team assigned to this duty. I can't tell you anything more because I don't know any more."

"It sounds like an important duty, indeed."

"Are you up to the job, son?"

John tried to lift his ears a teeny bit higher. "Yes, sir, I believe I am."

"Good," the major said. "Now, if you are related to Adam Ulnar, then you must also be related to his nephew, Captain Eric Ulnar."

"That is correct, sir."

"You will be serving under Captain Ulnar. He is waiting to meet with you at Green Hall. Gather your things and be on Landing Platform A-Thirty-one in fifty-five minutes. Is that understood?"

"Yes, sir."

"Good luck to you, Lieutenant."

"Thank you, sir."

John gave a salute with his right front paw. Major Stell returned the salute with his right hand.

After leaving the administrative building, John trotted eagerly across the Academy campus. The yellow globe of the sun burned brightly, its rays seeping warmly through John's fur. Almost every day at the Academy was sunny because it was located on an island just off the coast of California.

John hurried past the silvery Academy buildings. Finally, he came to a rocky cliff overlooking the sea. Far below, the ocean's waves broke rhythmically against the white, sandy beach.

John's ears, which were very sharp, picked up the distant roar of the surf and the screech of the seagulls. His black nose, which was also very sharp, took in the water's salty scent.

John wiped away a tear with his paw. He had

spent five wonderful years at this place, and he knew it might be quite a while before he ever saw it again. Indeed, he might even be leaving the planet Earth for a long period of time.

John also felt a painful sadness about leaving the many fine friends and instructors he had met at the Academy. But John knew there was no time for lengthy good-byes. It was time to pack his belongings—clothing, equipment, weapons, grooming supplies, chew toys— and report for his first tour of military duty.

Soon John was perched in the passenger seat of a small strato-flier, a ship designed to fly only within the Earth's atmosphere. Traveling twice the speed of sound, John gazed out the circular window, known as a porthole. His tongue was panting with pleasure.

John had studied many subjects at the Academy— leadership, astronomy, biology, physics, math, engineering, wilderness survival, self-defense, weaponry—but his favorite subject was flying. John had become the finest pilot in his class, and he hoped his duty would involve many flying missions— especially in outer space.

After a twenty-minute journey, the flier was soaring over the sun-baked desert of New Mexico. In the distance, John glimpsed a speck of green, glimmering against the ground like a precious emerald. John knew this was Green Hall, the capital of the Green Government.

Just the sight of the place caused John's ears to lift high with a sense of patriotism. The young officer loved Green Hall and all the great ideals it symbolized.

The Green Government was a democracy—a

government that was run by the people who lived under it. Its leaders were chosen in fair elections, and every person over the age of eighteen had the right to vote. The goals of the government were peace, equality, and freedom. John believed in these ideals and he was even willing to die for them. He hoped, of course, that would never be necessary.

As the strato-flier slowed and lowered, John got a look at Green Hall. It was a huge group of buildings, all made of brilliant green glass. In the center of the complex, a series of landing platforms towered two thousand feet up in the air. This was where the flying vehicles landed and took off. The complex was surrounded by a square mile of green parkland.

When the strato-flier landed, John was met by two Legion commandos in gray jumpsuits. The commandos were the common soldiers of the Legion. The men escorted John down an elevator, along several hallways, up another elevator, and along another hallway. A door automatically opened, and John stepped through, into a room.

Across the room, a tall man stood with his back to John. He was gazing out the window at the scenery.

John raised his ears to attention. "Lieutenant John Ulnar reporting for duty, sir."

The man at the window turned around. He was something to see. Beneath the navy jumpsuit, his body seemed to be in perfect condition. The features of his face were so sharp that they might have been cut from stone. The man's bright-yellow hair flowed to his shoulders. He looked more like a movie star than an officer of the Legion.

The man ran his eyes along John's furred body.

"So you are John Ulnar. I understand you are a relative of mine. A *distant* relative, of course."

"Yes, sir," John agreed. "I am a distant relative of yours."

John knew this was Eric Ulnar, because he had seen many three-dimensional pictures of the man in the news-puters and tele-screens. Though only thirty-three, he was quite famous. A few months earlier, Eric had led the very first expedition beyond the Earth's Solar System.

Eric and his fellow explorers had set foot on a planet that revolved around the star closest to Earth, Alpha Centauri. It turned out to be a dead planet, meaning no life-forms lived there. However, there must have been something very dangerous about the planet, because two-thirds of Eric's soldiers had died on the mission. The full details had never been made public.

"It's an honor to meet you, sir," John said proudly. "You are something of a legend among the students at the Legion Academy."

Eric gave a toss of his blond hair. "That pleases me. I enjoy being a legend."

This guy seems a little conceited, John thought, keeping himself at attention. *And I'm willing to bet he dyes that hair. But, then, great men are often pretty stuck on themselves.*

Eric took a seat in a leather chair and picked a green grape from a bowl.

Watching the grape, John felt his mouth water. John had a weakness for food. No matter how much John had eaten recently, he always wanted more.

Eric twirled the grape between his fingers. "Lieutenant, I'll be honest. I do not believe you are experienced enough for this assignment. However, my uncle, Adam Ulnar, insisted I use you. Since he is not only my uncle, but also the Supreme Commander of the Legion, I suppose it is my duty to follow his orders—just as I will expect you to follow *my* orders."

"Of course, sir."

"Excellent," Eric said, tossing the grape in John's direction.

John ran to the grape and instantly gobbled it. Then John looked at Eric, waiting patiently for either more information or more grapes.

"As you know," Eric said, after swallowing several grapes himself, "our mission is to guard the Keeper of AKKA. However, I cannot give you any more information until our ship has left Earth. In one hour and forty-five minutes, you are to be at Landing Platform G-Fourteen. That is all for now."

John gave a salute with his right front paw. Eric returned the salute with a lazy movement.

John hurried out of the building and paid a visit to the park surrounding Green Hall. After taking care of some necessary business at a tree, John gazed up at the blue sky.

Indeed, it seems I will be leaving Earth for a while. But where am I going? It could be almost anywhere in the Solar System. A space station, a planet, a moon, an asteroid. Who knows? I might even be going to some totally unknown part of our galaxy.

John Ulnar's tail went wagging with uncontrollable excitement. It didn't really matter where he went. He was about to fulfill his boyhood dream. His life as a soldier in the Legion of Space was about to begin!

WISHBONE'S GUIDE TO THE GALAXY

Hey, space is an awfully big place, and I wouldn't want anyone getting lost out there. So here are a few terms to help you find your way.

asteroid belt   a collection of rocky bodies, known as asteroids, located between Mars and Jupiter

atmosphere   a layer of skylike gases that surrounds a planet

extravehicular activity (EVA)   space-walking

five-degree-of-freedom chair (5DF)   a simulator used to re-create the weightlessness encountered on space-walks

galaxy   a collection of stars. Earth is located at the outer edge of a galaxy known as the Milky Way. There are believed to be many millions of galaxies in the universe, each containing many millions of stars.

gravity   a force that causes stars, planets, moons, and other bodies to be attracted to one another

light-year   the distance light travels in a year. A single light-year equals almost six trillion miles!

manned   a motorized backpack used for control-

maneuvering unit (MMU)
ling movements while space-walking

moon
a body that revolves around a planet. Some planets have no moons, and some planets have many of them.

multi-axis trainer (MAT)
a simulator used to re-create the sensation of a space vehicle spinning out of control

National Aeronautics and Space Administration (NASA)
since 1958, the organization in charge of the entire U.S. space program

one-sixth chair
a simulator used to re-create the gravity conditions of the moon

planet
a body that revolves around a star. It is not known what percentage of stars have planets around them.

rocket
a device that shoots forward by the use of explosive power

simulator
a device or vehicle used for training purposes

solar system
a collection of planets, moons, and other objects that revolve, or orbit, around a star. Earth's solar system is composed of nine planets and at least sixty-one moons.

space shuttle   the type of vessel currently used in U.S. missions into space. It consists of three basic parts: The *Orbiter* carries passengers and cargo. The solid rocket boosters (SRBs) propel the craft halfway to space. And the external tank (ET) propels the craft the rest of the way into space.

star   a large body in space made up of violently hot gas. Stars are the biggest objects that exist.

sun   an average-sized star that is the centerpiece of Earth's solar system

terra-form   to make a planet or moon livable for humans by re-creating Earthlike conditions

universe   all of space and everything it contains. It is thought to have begun about fifteen billion years ago. The size of the universe is totally unknown, but let's just say that it's *very big!*

warping   a technique that allows a vehicle to move through space at great speeds by curving the surface of space. So far, the idea of warping space is theoretical and appears only in stories and our imaginations.

CHAPTER THREE

John sat in a Legion spaceship as it rocketed through one hundred miles of the Earth's atmosphere. Out of the porthole, he saw the view change from light blue to dark blue and finally blackness. In less than a minute, the ship had entered space.

Space never failed to fill John with awe. Space began where the Earth's atmosphere ended and went on for . . . well . . . no one really knew. Its vastness couldn't even be imagined, let alone measured. Most of space was so empty of anything that it was colored a black deeper than any other black. Indeed, space was so empty, it was absolutely silent. And yet, space contained everything in the universe, everything that had ever been created.

It's a frontier that can never be fully explored, John thought, as he pressed his muzzle against the porthole. *A mystery that can never be fully solved. Perhaps that's why it fascinates me so much.*

As the ship made a wide turn, John saw Earth hovering in the blackness like a beautiful balloon. Across the curving surface, the blue of the oceans was broken up by tan and green patches of land. Fleecy white clouds drifted over the planet as if they were guardian angels.

John waved a paw. *Farewell, old friend. Don't worry, I'll be back.*

John's seat-straps opened automatically. John would have floated weightlessly out of his seat if it were not for the ship's artificial-gravity system. It kept the cabin's gravity exactly the way it would have been on Earth.

You know about gravity, right? It's that strange force that pulls downward and makes things have weight. The amount of gravity on Earth seems normal to us. Other planets and moons have different amounts of gravity, depending upon their size. In outer space, everything is totally weightless, because there is almost no gravity there. Okay, folks, let's keep traveling.

The cheerful male voice of the ship's computer made an announcement. "Our ship is now flying at ten thousand times the speed of sound. We expect to travel the forty-eight million miles to Mars in just under seven hours."

John's ears perked up. *Ah, so that's our destination. Mars. Nice planet.*

John had seen a bit of the Solar System in his twenty-one years. He had once vacationed on Mercury's moon, at a resort that advertised itself as having the beaches closest to the sun. He had flown several training missions to Venus, a strange world where there was constant thunder and lightning, but never a drop of rain. He had also visited Luna, Earth's moon, and Mars, both of which had many people living on them.

John looked over at Eric Ulnar, who was admiring

his flowing blond hair in a mirror. *This guy is more concerned with his appearance than a dog-show champion. He's a legend, all right, but I'm not so sure I like him.*

"Captain," John said, "can you tell me what part of Mars we will be stationed on?"

"The northern desert," Eric said, keeping his eyes on the mirror. "That's where the Keeper of AKKA is currently located. Every few months the Keeper is moved to a different secret location."

"Well, since we're on the subject, can you tell me now what AKKA is?"

"It's a very important weapon," Eric said, adjusting a lock of hair. "Your assignment doesn't require you to know any more than that."

John shifted the position of his tail to get more comfortable. He took a quick glance at two men who sat nearby. They were the other two guards who would be on Eric's guard team. One was a short fellow named Vors, a man who resembled a sneaky rat. The other was a tall fellow named Kimplen, a man who resembled a greedy wolf. They were both much older than John, both experienced Legion officers.

Using a remote control, Kimplen turned on the tele-screen that hung at the front of the cabin. A three-dimensional image of a comedian appeared. The man was cracking jokes about some politician from one of Jupiter's moons. Kimplen flipped through some channels, stopping when he came to the noisy roar of a professional laserball game.

"Hey, put it back," Vors whined. "I like that comedian."

"Yeah . . . well, I've got a bet riding on this game," Kimplen grumbled. "So, too bad."

Again John pressed his muzzle against the porthole. He saw stars gleaming in the deep, deep blackness of space. There were billions of them, too many for anyone ever to count. In space they appeared far more clear and wondrous than they did when viewed from Earth. Each star glittered as if it were a chipped piece of a diamond.

John picked out Sirius, the brightest star in this part of the galaxy. It was also known as the "dog star" because it was one of several stars that formed the shape of a dog. For some reason, Sirius had always been John's favorite star.

Yes, it's really happening, John thought, as he watched Sirius's radiant glow. *I am finally on a mission as a member of the Legion of Space!*

John thought of the Legion of Space as being much like the knights of King Arthur's Round Table— a brave band of soldiers traveling the land, making sure that good triumphed over evil. However, the Legion soldiers weren't galloping on horseback across the English countryside. They were zooming in spaceships through the vast black oceans of the universe.

John wished his parents could see him now, but they had passed away when John was just a young boy. John had spent most of his youth living with his mother's sister, a poor but very loving woman.

The fact was, John's family, the Ulnars, had played an important role in the history of the Solar System. Way back in the twenty-first century, one of John's ancestors, Mary Ulnar, had been a member of the first human voyage to Mars. Over the next several hundred years, other Ulnar ancestors had played key roles in the exploration and colonization of the System.

Perhaps the most important of these ancestors

was Zane Ulnar. In the twenty-fourth century, Zane Ulnar had invented a new type of nuclear-powered engine. This engine allowed ships to travel at speeds much greater than before. Suddenly it wasn't so difficult to journey to all points of the System.

This invention also had made Zane Ulnar very wealthy. The money was invested in various businesses and passed on from generation to generation. Before long, the Ulnars became the System's richest and most influential family.

John's ears drooped, remembering how history then took a dark turn.

In the twenty-sixth century, the five most powerful nations had taken part in World War III. Many Triple-H bombs were dropped, causing tremendous damage on Earth and elsewhere. When the smoke cleared from World War III, the System was divided into many weakened nations. As a result, space exploration came almost to a complete halt.

An ancestor named Alexander Ulnar saw this situation as a golden opportunity. He bought himself a vast force of warriors. Then he launched the War of Control, in which Alexander's forces went about conquering every single nation in the System. When the smoke had cleared, the victorious Alexander crowned himself Alexander I, Emperor of the Sun. When he died, he passed the title on to his eldest daughter, who was even more power-hungry than her father.

For almost two hundred years, the Ulnars had ruled the System with an iron fist. They became known as the Purple Empire, because purple was Alexander's favorite color.

It was a time much like the Dark Ages that began back in the fifth century. The royal family and a few favored others enjoyed great wealth, while all the rest of humanity was terribly poor. If any person or group dared to challenge the authority of the Purples, they were executed or sentenced to life in prison. For most people, it was a time of cruelty, suffering, and despair.

Finally, brave men and women throughout the System joined together, and so began what became known as the Great Revolution. The revolutionaries didn't have much money, but they did have the finest leaders and thinkers on their side. Fierce battles were fought all across the System against the mighty Purple warriors. This time when the smoke cleared, the Purples were thrown off the throne.

The revolutionaries united every part of the System into a single, democratic government. It was called the Green Government, after the precious greenery of life-giving plants. For the past two hundred years, the Green Government had ruled the System with wisdom, fairness, and peace. The Legion of Space was created to make sure things stayed that way.

No doubt about it, I have an interesting bloodline, John thought.

John had always had mixed feelings about being an Ulnar. On the one paw, he felt deep shame at the "purple streak" in his blood. On the other paw, he felt deep pride in the many great persons from his family's past.

John turned his attention back to the black world outside the porthole.

After less than seven hours of travel, the cheerful computer announced, "We are approaching our destination. Please be in your seat."

Automatically, straps crisscrossed John's furred body. Looking out the porthole, John saw the planet Mars come into view. Most of the surface was covered with greenery and wide canals of water.

Soon the ship was flying over Wells-Port, one of the largest cities in the System. John gave his tail a wag, remembering how he and some of his Academy buddies had once spent a fun-filled weekend in that most lively of towns.

Just think, hundreds of years ago, humans lived only on Earth.

The fact was, humans had spread themselves across the Solar System not just for the sake of science or excitement. It had been a necessity.

In the twenty-third century, Earth grew so crowded that there was not enough room or natural resources for all its population. So humans began to colonize various planets and moons throughout the System, starting with Luna and Mars.

Because Earth was the only body in the System naturally suited to life, the other planets and moons required much work to make them livable. They all needed four things added: Earthlike gravity, water, oxygen, and a comfortable temperature. All this was done through a process known as "terra-forming."

The Earthlike gravity was created with the help of massive generators. The water was either shipped in or made by melting existing areas of ice. The oxygen and temperature were controlled by introducing all sorts of Earth plants and animals into the environments, a process that took many decades. On the harsher planets and moons, additional machinery was needed to control the oxygen and temperature.

By the twenty-seventh century, the majority of

the bodies in the System were lived on by humans. However, the list did not include the largest planets—Jupiter, Saturn, Uranus, and Neptune. These planets were just giant balls of gas.

As the ship flew to the other side of Mars, day darkened into night. The ship began soaring over a stretch of desert that looked like the deserts of New Mexico. Finally, the ship landed right beside an ancient fort that had been used by the Russians in World War III. With its rugged walls built from volcano rock, it looked much like a castle that one of King Arthur's knights might have visited.

"We have reached our destination," the cheerful computer announced as the seat-straps opened. "You may now exit the ship."

"Don't mind if I do," John said, leaping off his seat.

John, Eric, Vors, and Kimplen left the ship and entered the fort. As the ship's crew unloaded supply crates, four other Legion soldiers boarded the ship.

They were the team being relieved by Eric's team, headed back to Earth.

An Asian woman approached, exchanging salutes with Eric. She was Captain Otan, the officer in charge of the guard team that would be sharing duty with Eric's team.

"Welcome to Mars," Captain Otan told the men. "My team is on duty now. Your team will take over tomorrow morning at oh-seven-hundred-forty-eight. I'll have someone show you to your quarters. Then we'll get some dinner for you fellows."

"Thanks," Eric said, giving Captain Otan a friendly slap on the back.

Ah, yes, dinner, John thought, as he licked his chops. *Space travel really makes my appetite take off.*

After a delicious dinner of steak and grilled potatoes, John entered his private room. It was a small space with stone walls and a single window. Dog-tired from a long day, John peeled off his jumpsuit and leaped onto his bed. Soon the young officer was fast asleep.

John's mind eased into a pleasant dream in which he was chasing a cat across the surface of Mars. The cat scampered up a tree, believing it was safe. But the cat didn't know that John was wearing a rocket pack on his back. As John zoomed upward, the cat stared with disbelief.

John opened an eye, realizing he was awake.

The tip of his tail was bristling, the way it did when his secret sense told him some kind of creature was watching him. John lifted his head and looked around. He neither saw, heard, nor smelled anything out of the ordinary.

Then his eyes fell on the window. Through the pane of duro-glass, John noticed something hovering in the night's blackness.

It was an eye.

A gigantic eye. Perhaps fifteen inches across. Oval-shaped. Liquidlike. Colored a strange shade of purple. A large black pupil in the center. The awful thing was staring directly at John. Not budging, not blinking. Showing only a blank stare.

Who—or what—is watching me?

There were no alien creatures anywhere in the System. Thus far, the only creatures humans had ever come into contact with were of the kinds that had originated on Earth. As far as John knew, none of those creatures possessed an eye this large.

The gigantic purple eye kept staring.

John felt something creep through every inch of his fur. It was *fear*—a fear so overwhelming that John couldn't hide or fight or flee or even bark out for help. He was frozen on his bed.

I've always thought of myself as a fearless man. And yet . . . now . . . I am afraid. Very afraid. Come on, John. Where's your courage? Snap out of it!

John forced himself to turn away and blink hard several times. Then he forced himself to face the window again.

The eye had vanished.

It took several hours before John managed to fall back asleep.

Okay, things are getting just a bit creepy on Mars. How about a quick trip back to Earth?

Chapter Four

Night had fallen on the U.S. Space & Rocket Center grounds. Wishbone and his fellow team members stood outside in Shuttle Park, which was just a short distance from Rocket Park. The trainees were looking up at a giant spaceship that was perched off the ground in a horizontal position.

There were three big rockets—two white ones, and a really jumbo one that was dark orange. Riding on top of the rockets was a white vehicle that looked much like a jet airplane. The spaceship was bathed in a soft glow of light that made it look like a futuristic ghost.

This was a full-scale model of the space shuttle, about which the trainees had just heard a lecture in the auditorium. Wishbone knew this was the type of vehicle currently used by NASA for space travel.

"Wow!" Joe said, gazing up at the shuttle. "Would I like to go on one of those!"

"And I'd like to go with you," Wishbone told Joe.

Several other trainees expressed their desire to take a trip on the shuttle.

Monique, the counselor, glanced up at the sky,

where a sprinkling of stars glittered. "I guess the stars are listening. Because, in a way, you trainees will get your wish this week. As part of your training, the Charger team will execute two simulated shuttle missions. They won't be real missions, of course, but they will be pretty close. On each mission, some of you will be part of the ground crew, and the rest of you will be part of the flight crew."

Wishbone pawed eagerly at Joe's leg. "Hey, do you hear that, Joe? We're going into space! Me and you!"

Monique led the team along a sidewalk back to the Habitat. Everyone went inside and gathered in a circle on the carpeted floor. Sitting beside Joe, Wishbone examined the Habitat more closely.

The building's high-tech interior was mostly white, accented here and there with bold splashes of red, yellow, and blue. There was a central corridor that

was open all the way up to the four-story ceiling. Catwalks with metal railings ran around the upper floors, and several stairways connected the different levels. Wishbone figured this was all in keeping with the "space station" design.

Wishbone noticed that everything was identified by a sign with a "space station" name. For example, windows were "Earth Study Portholes," water fountains were "H_2O Dispensers," and bathrooms were "Waste-Management Units."

Speaking of bathrooms, it's too bad they don't have a tree or fire hydrant in here. Oh, well, I'll figure something out.

In a welcoming way, Monique asked each of the trainees to tell the others a little about themselves. Wishbone raised his ears, listening with interest.

The Charger team consisted of nine boys, seven girls, and one dog. They came from all over the country, some from big cities, some from tiny towns. Several of the trainees had come on scholarships sponsored by schools or local clubs. A few of the others had earned their tuition, the way Sam and David had done. One girl was treated to her tuition by her parents because she hadn't gotten in trouble for five years.

Five years! I have a tough time going five days without getting into some *kind of trouble.*

Introductions over, Monique explained all the positions available for the team's two shuttle missions. Then she passed out forms, on which the trainees were to list their first, second, and third choice for what positions they wanted. The forms also contained questions—some about the space program, some about personal matters.

The trainees spread out and spent some time wrestling with their decisions.

Kelsey, a tall girl who was in love with Captain Kirk from the old *Star Trek* series, raised her hand. "Who does more flying? The commander or the pilot?"

"They both fly, but the commander does a little more," Monique answered. "The commander is really the pilot, and the pilot is really the copilot. They just use those terms because none of the astronauts wanted to be called a copilot. Call it astronaut ego."

Joe, Sam, David, and Wishbone huddled together. For some reason, Wishbone wasn't given a form, but he looked over at Joe's form.

"What are you guys going for?" Sam asked her friends.

"As first choice," Joe said confidently, "I'm going for the flight's commander."

"You'd be a great commander," Sam remarked.

"I'm a science guy," David said, writing on his form. "So I'm taking payload specialist for first choice. They do all sorts of cool experiments during the flight."

"What about you, Sam?" Joe asked.

Sam stared at her form. "Hmm . . . I think I'll take mission specialist for first choice. They get to space-walk. I can't think of anything neater than that."

Wishbone gave his side a thoughtful scratch. *Let's see. What position do I most want? I wouldn't mind being commander, but then I don't want to compete with Joe. I think I'll take pilot as first choice. With Joe and me flying the ship, the mission will be in good paws.*

After the trainees handed in their forms, Monique addressed the team. "Now we need to design a mission patch. In the U.S. space program, there's a long tradition of crews designing patches that they wear during their flight. The patch can show whatever you want, but you need to give it a theme."

Wishbone noticed a trainee named Andy staring at him. Andy, the youngest in the group, was a round-faced sixth-grader from South Carolina. Sixth-graders were allowed to attend the Space Academy only if they had already attended Space Camp, which Andy had. Of all the team, Andy had the most serious desire to become a real astronaut.

Finally, Andy spoke in his polite Southern accent. "Well, Wishbone is here to honor Laika, the dog who went into space. So in honor of both Wishbone and Laika, why don't we put a dog on our patch?"

Everyone greeted the idea with great enthusiasm.

Wishbone tilted his head modestly. "Guys, I really couldn't accept such an honor. However . . . if you insist . . . well, all right."

Sam volunteered to draw the patch in her spare time. Then everyone spent some time discussing the patch's design. Some great ideas were tossed about, and the experience helped to get the group working as a team.

You know, Wishbone thought, looking at the six-teen boys and girls around him, *I'm growing to like my team quite a bit. They have excellent taste. Ah . . . speaking of taste, I could use a snack right about now.*

10:30 P.M. Wishbone lay at the foot of Joe's bed in their room on the fourth floor of the Habitat. The lights had just been turned out. But Wishbone, Joe, and the five other boys in the room were too keyed up to go right to sleep.

"What's Oakdale like?" the boy in the bunk above Joe asked. This was Jordan, a husky, outgoing boy.

"Most of the time it's a quiet town," Joe replied.

"But every now and then, some pretty interesting things happen. What's it like in Vermont?"

"It's great if you like skiing and maple syrup," Jordan said. "Fortunately, I love both. Hey, Robert, how do you like living in San Antonio, Texas?"

Robert, a quiet Hispanic boy, said, "It's pretty cool. But I haven't been to many other places so it's hard to compare."

Twenty minutes later, the voices drifted off and all six boys were sound asleep. Wishbone, however, kept shifting positions and digging at the covers with his paws.

I can't get to sleep, for some reason. I think I'm nervous. Yes, that's it. I'm nervous about being the first dog to go through Space Academy. After all, that's an awfully big responsibility. Because if I do well, then other dogs might be invited into the program, and that might lead to NASA creating a whole new breed of astrodogs.

But am I up to the task? Can I handle the pressure? Do I have the right stuff? To be honest . . . I don't know.

John Ulnar is about to have his "right stuff" tested in a big way. Yup, things are about to get very strange and dangerous on Mars.

CHAPTER FIVE

The dawn sky on Mars was an enchanting blend of grapefruit pink and lemonade yellow.

John galloped across the ground, about a mile from the fort, his paws stirring up flurries of red dust. The young officer always liked to catch a little exercise first thing in the morning.

Though John remembered the gigantic purple eye he had seen the night before, he no longer feared it. John had come to realize that the frightening eye was nothing more than a harmless nightmare.

It frequently happens when I'm sleeping in a new bed, John thought, as he slowed to a stop.

John admired the Martian landscape. The rocky desert stretched for miles in every direction, the ground colored a rusty red. Off in the distance a volcano towered to the sky, clouds of mist hovering around its peak.

John wandered over to a sand dune and did his usual fifteen minutes of digging exercise. When he had made a nice hole, John pulled a bone from his back pocket that he had saved from the previous night's dinner. He dropped the bone in the hole, then turned around to cover it over with his back paws.

Ah, now I feel at home on Mars. Well, I'd better get back to the fort in time for breakfast!

At 07:48, Captain Ulnar's team began their guard duty. John, Vors, and Kimplen were instructed to keep a close watch on the Keeper at all times. Each of the soldiers wore a proton pistol on his belt, a weapon that fired deadly electromagnetic rays.

John, Vors, and Kimplen went to the fort's courtyard, where they took over for the three guards working under Captain Otan. The courtyard was a square area surrounded by rocky walls.

"I'm eager to get a look at this Keeper," John told Vors and Kimplen. "Where is he? I don't see him yet."

The wolflike Kimplen pointed. "The Keeper is right over there. The prettiest flower in the garden."

John's eyes followed Kimplen's finger to a corner of the courtyard. A garden lay there, filled with colorful flowers. Among the flowers, John noticed a lovely young woman kneeling. She looked to be in her early twenties, not much older than John himself.

John's ears shifted with confusion. *I didn't expect someone so young, so soft, so . . . beautiful. What a lonely life she must lead. Always moving from place to place. Unable to stay close to her friends and family. Knowing she—and she alone—keeps the secret of AKKA. A secret so important that the safety of the Green Government depends upon it.*

"Come on, Vors. Let's play a hand of cards."

"Sure, Kimplen. How about a game of Demon Eyes? Jokers are wild."

Vors and Kimplen sat on a stone bench and began playing cards. John found this odd, considering the guards were supposed to be watching the Keeper's every move. But he figured the experienced soldiers knew what they were doing.

As for John, he didn't mind watching the Keeper. And he did just that. After several minutes, the young woman began watching John back.

Finally, the Keeper called to John, "Oh, sir, could you lend me a hand, please?"

John didn't see any harm in this. So he trotted over to the flower garden.

"Hello," the Keeper said, a voice that sounded like music.

Up close, she was a vision of loveliness. Her slender figure was draped in a short, simple garment of white fabric. Her hair glowed a glorious mixture of red, brown, and gold. Her smooth face was highlighted by steady, honest, gray eyes that seemed to mirror her soul.

John raised his ears, trying to appear as handsome and manly as possible. "Hello. I am one of the guards on Captain Ulnar's team. My name is John."

"My name is Aladoree."

John gave himself a bashful paw scratch. "It is indeed a pleasure to meet you."

"I've been keeping an eye on you since you arrived last night," Aladoree told John. "I'm a good judge of character. You seem to be a faithful member of the Legion."

"That I am," John said, lifting his ears a bit higher. "But I thought I was supposed to be the one keeping an eye on *you*."

Aladoree lowered her voice to a whisper. "I wish to confide in you, sir. But I don't want those other men to know I am doing so. Pretend you are only

helping me with my gardening. As you can see, I've managed to grow gardenias, daffodils, and magnolias here. Now I'm trying my hand with tulips. You dig the holes, and I will drop in the bulbs."

"As it so happens," John remarked, "digging holes is one of my specialties."

Aladoree pointed to a spot on the ground.

John set his front paws to work and said, "What do you wish to tell me?"

"I fear there is treachery close by."

"Treachery?"

"Do you understand the importance of AKKA?"

"I know that it's a very important weapon. But no one has told me what it is exactly."

"I am going to tell you now. You understand, this is top-secret information."

John stopped digging. "I understand."

Aladoree dropped a bulb into the fresh hole. "Very few people know the true story of how the Great Revolution was won. It's not something that made it into the public history records."

"What is the true story?" John asked, as he covered the hole over with his back paws.

"During that time," Aladoree continued, "there lived a man named Charles Anthar. Not only was he a brilliant physicist, but he was also a champion of liberty. Before the revolution, he was sentenced to life in prison on Pluto for daring to criticize the Purple emperor. While in prison, he designed a new type of weapon. It was more powerful than any weapon mankind has yet known."

"How horrible," John said, as he began digging a new hole.

"But this weapon was built for the sake of freedom," Aladoree explained. "During the revolution, some of the revolutionaries managed to break Charles Anthar out of prison. He built this weapon and demonstrated its power to the Purple emperor. When the emperor saw the weapon's enormous power, he surrendered. That is the real story of how the revolution was won."

John stopped digging. "Let me guess. That weapon is AKKA."

"Yes," Aladoree said, dropping a bulb in the hole. "You see, AKKA allowed the birth of the Green Government. And as long as the Green Government has AKKA, they will continue in peace—that is, as long as no one else gets the secret of AKKA."

"I see."

Aladoree's eyes shone with nobility. "To protect the secret, Charles Anthar decided that only one living person at a time should know how to build AKKA. Shortly before Charles died, he passed the secret on to one of his relatives. And so it has been passed on through the years. My full name is Aladoree Anthar. I am an ancestor of Charles Anthar. I received the secret of AKKA from my father six years ago, right before he died."

John covered over the hole. "Is the secret written down anywhere?"

"No. It is kept only in my mind. But I can build the weapon very quickly out of the most simple materials."

"This is most fascinating. But why have you told me this information?"

"As you must know," Aladoree said, leaning close to John, "Eric Ulnar is descended from the family of Ulnar emperors and empresses. I have always kept a close watch on the Ulnars, knowing some of them would one day seek to regain their throne. As soon as I learned Eric was to be the captain of the new guard team, I grew suspicious. Why would a famous explorer like him want this assignment?"

"Surely you don't suspect Eric Ulnar of treachery?"

"That's exactly what I suspect," Aladoree said, picking up a water container. "I believe he wants to kill or kidnap me so the Green Government will no longer have access to AKKA. That, of course, would make it possible for him to attack the Green Government with a chance of success. And I suspect the other two guards on your team are part of Eric's plan."

"No, you've got it wrong," John declared. "Eric may be a bit stuck on himself, but I am sure he is no traitor. After all, many fine men and women have been Ulnars, including Adam Ulnar, Supreme Commander of the Legion. Just because a person's last name is Ulnar doesn't mean he or she dreams of becoming an emperor or empress."

"I believe it does," Aladoree said coldly.

"I'll prove that you are wrong. My full name is John Ulnar."

"What?" Aladoree said with a look of horror. "You are descended from the royal family of Ulnars?"

"Yes, but you have nothing to fear from me."

"Oh, I was a fool to have confided in you," Aladoree said, backing away from John. "Now you will warn Eric that I am on to his evil scheme."

John raised a paw in protest. "No, I . . . listen . . . please, I mean no—"

"I can trust no one who goes by the name Ulnar," Aladoree said, a look of hatred shooting from her eyes. "Sir, farewell!"

Aladoree stalked away from John, moving to another part of the courtyard.

I suppose I understand why she's so mistrustful, John thought, as he licked some dirt from his paws. *After all, the lady holds the safety of the entire Solar System in her head.*

Hearing a beep, John pulled out a small device. Eric's face appeared on a tiny screen, saying, "John, come to the quarters of Captain Otan. At once."

"Yes, sir," John replied.

Moments later, John met Eric in Captain Otan's room. John's fur bristled when he saw Captain Otan crumpled on the floor.

Eric wore a serious expression. "She has been killed by a proton gun. I suspect the murderer is one of the three guards on her team. I want you to find these men at once and lock them away in the fort's prison."

John did not understand why any one of those men would have murdered their captain. Like a good soldier, however, he followed the order. Within twenty minutes, John had locked Captain Otan's three guards in the dreary underground prison.

Then the day turned even uglier. Hearing the whine of an engine, John raised himself up onto his hind legs to look out a window.

He saw a terra-sled racing away from the fort, rushing over the ground on a cushion of air. Four persons were riding the sled. The fur on John's back shot up when he realized who the four people were—Eric, Vors, Kimplen, and Aladoree!

I smell something rotten on the planet Mars. Aladoree must have been right about Eric. He is kidnapping her. Do something, John!

John ran down a flight of stone steps and bolted out the door of the fort. Though the terra-sled was no longer in view, John had seen in which direction it was headed, and he could follow the scent of its passengers. John raced along the rocky ground as fast as his four paws would carry him.

A mile later, John skidded to a stop. His lower jaw dropped open with amazement.

A vehicle stood on the rust-colored ground. It was unlike any vehicle John had ever seen. A big black ball, large enough to fit several hundred men inside, stood on six curving legs. The vehicle reminded John of a gigantic mechanical spider.

John spotted Eric, Vors, Kimplen, and Aladoree stepping onto a type of elevator that ran inside the vehicle. Vors and Kimplen were each holding one of Aladoree's arms. The elevator began to rise.

"Hold!" John called out. "Eric Ulnar, you are a

traitor to the Legion and to your government! I demand that you stop!"

The elevator paused about ten feet off the ground. Surprisingly, the athletic Eric jumped to the ground. He walked toward John, stopping just a few feet away.

"I demand to know what's going on," John told Eric.

"I am going on a trip with Vors, Kimplen, and Aladoree," Eric replied.

"In other words, you are kidnapping Aladoree. You are a traitor!"

Eric gave a proud toss of his blond hair. "I dislike that word *traitor*. Besides, it's not accurate. I prefer to think that I am reclaiming what rightfully belongs to my family—namely, the Purple Empire."

"You will fail," John insisted.

"I don't think so," Eric said with a slight smile. "Without Aladoree, the Green Government no longer has AKKA. That will make them easy enough to defeat."

John couldn't help but chuckle. "Is that so? Do you forget the Green Government is protected by the Legion of Space? It's the strongest, fastest, most well-trained fighting force ever established."

"Yes, but I have the Medusas."

John felt his whiskers twitch. "Who are the Medusas?"

"Intelligent creatures from a distant planet," Eric said in a matter-of-fact manner. "Well, I call them Medusas. I have no idea what they call themselves. I met these creatures when I made that expedition beyond Earth's solar system. Of course, I never made that information public. Now you understand why."

John pawed at the ground, wrestling with this

incredible information. *So it has finally happened. Humans have made contact with alien creatures. Intelligent ones, at that. This is . . . very big news. Keep your cool, John. Just as you were trained to do at the academy.*

John pointed his muzzle toward the spidery vehicle. "I suppose that ship belongs to these so-called Medusas."

"Yes," Eric replied. "And the Medusas have agreed to assist me in my effort to reclaim the Purple Throne. You see, they have a technology even more advanced than ours. Take this ship, for example. It landed last night, but Captain Otan saw no trace of it on the radar screen. Do you know why that is? Because the ship *teleported* here."

This was more big news for John. Scientists had long dreamed of teleporting. Simply put, teleporting meant to break down all the atoms of a person or object until that person or object disappeared. Then the atoms were *transferred* somewhere else, allowing the person or object to suddenly reappear in a completely different place—even if that place was many millions of miles away.

"Why are the Medusas helping you?" John asked.

"They need iron," Eric explained. "A mineral that is most useful for machinery. They have no iron in their solar system, but we have oodles of it in ours. I will be supplying them with iron in exchange for their help in battle. The Medusas also have some interest in getting the secret of AKKA from Aladoree. That's why we're kidnapping her instead of just killing her."

"Aladoree will never give away the secret of AKKA."

Eric shrugged. "I believe the Medusas may have some . . . effective methods of persuasion."

John bared his teeth in anger. "If anyone hurts that lady, so help me—"

"Easy, boy," Eric said with a laugh. "Though I must admit, the only reason I'm telling you this is to see your reaction. You look most amusing when you are upset."

"What happened to Captain Otan?" John growled.

"I murdered her," Eric said casually. "Why? So you would lock up the three men on her guard team. This would keep you and them out of my hair while I, Vors, and Kimplen made off with Aladoree. By the way, what did you think of my acting when I was in Captain Otan's room?"

"Oh, you are an excellent liar, sir."

"Thank you. Sure, it would have been simpler just to kill all of you. However, my uncle would have been quite upset if I had caused your death."

John bent back his ears. "Your uncle is the Supreme Commander of the Legion. And I guarantee he will be quite upset about this whole thing!"

Eric released a high-pitched laugh that was almost girlish.

John sprang into the air, using a move he had perfected at the academy. After snatching the proton gun out of Eric's belt, John landed squarely on his four paws and aimed the gun at its owner. He was hoping to frighten, not kill, Eric.

Suddenly John turned, catching a sign of movement near the top of the spidery vehicle. John saw something. Or at least part of something. It was a big, greenish, jellylike glob—with a giant purple eye.

So that wasn't a nightmare last night!

As he had the night before, John felt his fur creep and crawl with an overwhelming sense of fear. The young officer was frozen in place, totally unable to move.

"Aahhh!!!"

John realized the scream was his own. His right front paw was stinging, as if acid were burning through it. The pistol had dropped to the ground. Obviously the "alien thing" had zapped John with some sort of weapon.

As Eric's hideous laugh grew louder, John felt himself going weak and shaky. In a fading voice, he muttered, "Eric Ulnar, I demand that you stop. You are a traitor to the . . ."

John lost his balance, tumbling to the ground. The whole world went black.

CHAPTER SIX

John opened his eyes slowly. The midday sun blazed into his face, and he felt a burning pain on his right front paw. Though painful, the injury didn't seem too serious.

What happened to me?

As John forced himself to stand, he began to remember the morning's terrible events—Eric kidnapping Aladoree; the creature with the purple eye; being zapped with a weapon.

John turned his muzzle in the direction where the alien space vehicle had stood. He saw nothing there except a cloud of blowing dust. The ship was gone. So were the Medusas, Eric, Vors, Kimplen . . . and Aladoree.

John dug a paw angrily at the ground. *If I had not frozen up with fear, I might have managed to save Aladoree. But now she's gone, and so is AKKA, and it's all my fault. In my first important moment as a soldier of the Legion, I have failed!*

John gave his body an energetic shake, the way he did right after a swim or bath.

Come on, there's no use crying about a knocked-over water bowl. I need to do something. Fast. But what? By now, Aladoree might be out of the Solar System. I know. I'll contact Adam Ulnar, the Supreme Commander of the Legion. If anyone needs to know about this, he's the one!

John ran back to the fort, where he sent an emergency message to the Legion's headquarters. He reported Aladoree's kidnapping, without mentioning Eric's role in it. A Legion captain promised to send a ship to Mars immediately. John knew the ship would come very soon because the headquarters were located on Phobos, a moon of Mars that was only several thousand miles away.

Within fifteen minutes, the ship landed. By that time, John had released the three guards he had wrongly imprisoned for the murder of Captain Otan. John and the three guards—Jay, Giles, and Samdu—boarded the ship, and the ship took off.

Soon John saw the tiny, potato-colored moon of Phobos come into view. With a shudder, John remembered that the name *Phobos* was Latin for *fear.*

Get hold of yourself. There is no time for fear now!

Soaring over Phobos, John saw a structure built of shimmering purple metal. This was Purple Palace, the former headquarters of the Purple Empire. Oddly enough, the building now served as the Legion headquarters.

When the Legion ship set down on a landing platform, the passengers were met by a group of Legion commandos. One of the commandos took charge of John, leading him through a series of luxurious hallways.

As he trotted along, John peeked through a partly open door. He caught sight of a vast room. A splendid throne floated magnetically off the ground, and it was decorated with priceless purple diamonds. John realized this used to be the throne room of the Purple emperors and empresses.

If I weren't so upset right now, I wouldn't mind taking a nice nap on that thing.

Soon the commando left John in the Supreme Commander's study. It looked more like a scholar's study than that of a military commander. One wall was crammed from floor to ceiling with books. And they weren't compu-books, where ten thousand titles could be stored on a single computer drive. They were books of the old-fashioned kind, with bindings, and pages of real paper. Being a book lover, John found these antique volumes of great interest.

A man looked down at John with piercing blue eyes. He wore the navy-blue jumpsuit of a Legion high officer. Despite his advanced age, the man seemed to be in excellent physical condition. His beard and mane of flowing hair were snow-white. The man gave off an air of confidence and knowledge that made John immediately trust him. John knew, of course, this was Adam Ulnar, the Supreme Commander of the Legion of Space.

Adam Ulnar gave a welcoming smile. "John Ulnar, I am most happy to see you."

John lifted his ears to full height. "It is an honor to meet you, sir."

Adam sat in a leather chair, gesturing for John to take a seat as well.

He doesn't seem too worried about losing the Keeper, John thought, as he sat on the floor. *Why not? Perhaps he is just keeping cool under pressure.*

Adam focused his eyes on John, studying the young officer. Yet he said nothing.

John gave his side a nervous paw scratch. "Uh . . . sir, I have never had the chance to thank you in person for helping me get into the Legion Academy. It seems you also got me the important job of protecting the Keeper of AKKA. Unfortunately—"

"Unfortunately," Adam said without a trace of anger, "it appears you have failed in that assignment."

John lowered his voice so the room's computer would not overhear the conversation. "Yes, I suppose I have failed. But there is something you need to know, sir. Your nephew, Eric, is the one responsible for Aladoree's disappearance. He has formed a partnership—"

Adam finished the thought. "—with the Medusas. And they are now on their way to the Medusas' home planet."

"Yes," John said, his ears shifting with confusion.

"But I don't understand how you know this already. It just happened, and I have not yet told anyone about Eric being mixed up in this."

"You see," Adam said calmly, "I knew about this even *before* it happened."

"Ah, sir," John said with relief, "I am glad to hear this. If you knew about this in advance, then I'm sure you have Legion soldiers on their way to capture Eric and rescue Aladoree."

"No, Eric will not be captured," Adam stated. "And Aladoree will not be rescued."

John was more puzzled than ever. "But . . . Eric is planning to crush the Green Government and bring back the Purple Empire. If we lose the power of AKKA, he may be able to do it—especially if he has the Medusas helping him."

A long pause followed.

Adam showed the ghost of a smile. "John, it was *my* idea to overthrow the Green Government. Eric is working with me."

"What?" John said, not believing his ears. "You mean . . . you are the mastermind of this evil scheme?"

Adam nodded his head.

This is most awful, John thought, his tail drooping with shock. *The Supreme Commander of the Legion no longer believes in the ideals of the Legion. It's like King Arthur suddenly turning over the Round Table and running off to fight alongside the bad guys. I . . . I . . . don't know what to do.*

Adam knelt beside John and scratched the back of John's right ear. "I'm sorry to have upset you. I had planned for you to learn about this in an easier way. Eric was supposed to bring Aladoree and you to Phobos. Then I would have explained everything to you. Hopefully, in a way that would have brought you over to our side."

"What happened?" John said, enjoying Adam's scratching, but not the words being spoken.

"The Medusas showed up at Eric's doorstep and insisted on taking Aladoree to their planet. They want to see if they can get the secret of AKKA from her, poor girl. I told Eric this was a bad idea, but apparently the Medusas would not take no for an answer."

John shuddered with a memory of the jellylike creature he had seen.

"To be honest," Adam said, now scratching the back of John's left ear, "I didn't want to form the partnership with the Medusas in the first place. We could have overthrown the Green Government without them. I have brought many Legion men and women on to my side. And, of course, I have access to most of the Legion vehicles and weaponry. But then Eric met the Medusas on that expedition and decided we would have a better chance of winning if we could call on their assistance. I suppose it will work out all right. But I have never met a Medusa, and I can't say I fully trust them."

"But why do you wish to overthrow the Green Government?" John said, pulling away from Adam. "You seem like such a reasonable fellow. Yet this plan is complete madness!"

Adam got up and began pacing the room, his manner becoming like that of a professor lecturing his students. "John, some believe the best method of government is a democracy, where every citizen has the right to vote for the leaders. Others believe the best method is a monarchy, where one person rules with absolute power—a king or czar or emperor. This is an argument that's been going on for thousands of years. I have come to the conclusion that a monarchy is the best method."

John raised a paw. "With all due respect, sir, you are wrong. When the Purple Empire ruled, there was no freedom. The royals and their friends lived the high life, while everyone else suffered."

Adam pushed a button, lighting up giant screens all around the room. The screens showed live images of all the planets and moons of the Solar System. It was like a stunning display of artwork, each planet and moon a totally different color and design.

"What you say is true," Adam told John. "They were not good emperors. But I believe there is such a thing as a good emperor. An emperor with the wisdom and kindness to run things in the best way possible. The great thinkers of ancient Greece called this kind of ruler a philosopher-king. When my family reclaims the throne, I will be this type of emperor."

"And when you pass away, who will take over as emperor?"

Adam stared at the screen showing the planet Saturn. It was called "the jewel of the System" for good reason. Multicolored rings of ice swirled around a globe colored a rich tone of gold.

"My only child passed away several years ago," Adam said softly. "So I was intending to pass the crown on to my nephew, Eric. But lately I've been reconsidering this move. Eric was spoiled as a little boy, and he is still spoiled. He acts too quickly, without considering the consequences of his actions."

"That's the problem with a monarchy," John pointed out. "Some emperors may be just fine. But

when you get a bad apple, it's extremely difficult to throw it away."

Adam spun around to face John. "However, I believe I can avoid the problem of Eric. Only a few moments ago, I realized there is an Ulnar far more qualified to follow me as Emperor of the Sun."

"Who?"

"You."

"*Me?!*" John exclaimed, his tail jumping with surprise.

"As you may recall," Adam continued, "I met you once when you were only a boy. Even then I could see the nobility in your eyes. When you approached manhood, I arranged for you to attend the Legion Academy. By that time, I was toying with the idea of renewing the Purple Empire, and I wanted you trained to assist with the takeover. I arranged for you to join Eric's guard team as a way of bringing you close to the action."

"I wish you had made some of this known to me," John said, moving away from Adam.

Adam knelt down to John. "Oh, John, my boy, as I look at you now, I still see that nobility in your eyes. And I know with all my heart that you would be the perfect person to succeed me as emperor. You have all the necessary qualities, and, what's more, you carry the royal blood of the Ulnars!"

John looked around at the screens. For a moment, he was dazzled into dizziness by the spectacular images of the planets and moons. John blinked hard, then faced the bearded man.

"There's only one problem," John said evenly. "I'm not interested in the job."

"Think of it, John," Adam said with great passion.

"All the wealth and power of the Solar System will be under your command. And you will be a brilliant emperor!"

"I said I'm not interested in the job," John insisted. "In fact, I hope for nothing more than a chance to smash your evil scheme!"

Adam pushed a button, causing all the screens to go blank.

"If you are against me," Adam said, returning calmly to his chair, "I fear you would be a powerful opponent. Yet, I confess, John, I like you too much to order your execution. Therefore, I give you a choice. Either accept my offer to become emperor of the Sun, or spend the rest of your life rotting in a dungeon. Which will you choose?"

John bent back his ears with determination. "I, too, know something about the great thinkers of ancient Greece. One of them was named Democritus. Indeed, the word *democracy* comes from his name. He said 'I would rather live poor in a democracy than be wealthy under the reign of a king.' And, sir, I feel exactly the same way!"

"So be it," Adam Ulnar said with piercing eyes. "We are now enemies."

"So be it," John Ulnar said, not backing down from the powerful man's gaze.

Wow, this plot is spinning faster than Saturn's rings! But before we go spinning off to who knows where, let's see how things are going back at the Space Academy.

CHAPTER SEVEN

Early Monday morning, Wishbone was awakened by a sharp knock on the door of his room in the Habitat. A voice called, "Rise and shine, trainees! Be ready for breakfast by eight!"

With a big yawn, Wishbone stretched his four paws. He noticed Joe and the other boys in the room going through a similar routine. Some of the boys headed for the showers, but Wishbone just scratched some dirt off his fur.

After an hour of get-ready time, the team was prepared for another day of Space Academy. All the other trainees wore the Space Academy T-shirts they had been given the day before. Wishbone, however, decided to stick with his fur coat.

The team was led to the cafeteria by their day counselor, Susan. Like Monique, she was in her twenties. Susan seemed a bit stricter than Monique, but Wishbone soon learned she could be counted on for an occasional joke or back scratch.

8:30 A.M. After the trainees ate breakfast, Susan led the Charger team into the Space & Rocket Center

69

museum. Open to the general public, the museum was located in a large building connected to the Space Camp Training Center.

The museum was a very big area, with dim, dramatic lighting. A hush surrounded the place, as there were no other visitors at this early hour. All around, Wishbone saw fascinating objects, mementos of mankind's adventures in space.

Susan spoke in a quiet but knowing voice. "For a long time, humans dreamed of going into space. But they didn't have the knowledge and technology to do it until the year 1957. That's when the space age began."

Hey, that was the year Laika went up.

As if she had heard his thoughts, Susan looked at Wishbone. "In that year, the Russians sent an unmanned satellite called *Sputnik* into space. Then they sent up a second *Sputnik*. This one carried a living creature, a mutt named Laika. Soon after, the Russians sent up a few more dogs. Around the same time, the United States sent up a few monkeys and chimps."

Wishbone looked up at Joe. "How did chimps and monkeys get into the space program?"

"In those days," Susan continued, "the U.S. and the Russians were enemies. So they were really trying to outdo each other in the space race. In 1961, the Russians sent the first man, Yuri Gagarin, into space. A few months later, the U.S. sent Alan Shepard into space."

Then Susan led the trainees around the museum, showing them various displays. All the while she talked about the history of man's exploration into space. Among the displays were: *Mercury, Gemini,* and *Apollo* capsules, just like the ones that had carried U.S. astronauts into space; a display showing mannequin astronauts and a lunar vehicle standing on a model of the moon's surface; and mock-ups of the *Skylab* and *Mir* space stations.

In addition to giving the trainees basic facts about everything, Susan usually threw in some funny details. Wishbone especially liked a story about how one of the *Gemini* astronauts smuggled a pastrami sandwich in a pocket of his spacesuit.

10:30 A.M. Susan took the Charger team to the Training Center, where she led them onto the training floor. This was the same huge area where the trainees had tried out the one-sixth chair the previous evening.

Susan stood beside a device that reminded Wishbone of a white easy chair. It was lifted several feet off the ground by a metal stand with a motor attached.

"This is an MMU simulator," Susan told the group. "That stands for 'manned maneuvering unit.' Does anyone know what an MMU is used for?"

"Space-walking!" several trainees called out.

Susan nodded. "As you know, sometimes astronauts go outside their vehicle and walk in space. The correct term for space-walking is extra-vehicular activity. For short, it's known as an EVA."

"I'm noticing that everything in the space program goes by its initials," Wishbone whispered to Sam. "NASA, MMU, EVA. Whatever happened to regular words?"

"Out in space, a person floats around weightlessly," Susan continued. "That's because there is almost no gravity in space. Sometimes the astronauts use MMUs, which are like big backpacks that help the astronauts control their movements."

"Got it," Wishbone said with a nod.

Going in alphabetical order, Susan called the first

trainee, David Barnes. After putting on a helmet, David climbed into the chair and Susan strapped him in place. Susan explained how to work the MMU's controls. Then she flipped a switch, causing a motor to whir.

"Now move yourself around," Susan instructed.

David turned a knob on the chair's arm, and the MMU went moving backward. Turning another knob,

David moved himself around in a slow circle. Wishbone could see that the manned maneuvering unit was traveling on a cushion of air that came from metal plates on the chair's stand.

"Try a tilt," Susan advised.

Turning another knob, David began tilting sideways. Over and over he went, until his feet were almost even with his head.

Suddenly, panic flickered in David's eyes.

Wishbone's tail twitched nervously. *Uh-oh, I think David's fear of heights just kicked in. He's only several feet off the ground, but for some people that can do the trick.*

David looked relieved when he climbed out of the chair several minutes later. Then the rest of the team tried the MMU, most of them enjoying their ride in the strange machine. For some reason, though, Wishbone wasn't given a chance to test out the chair.

Oh, well, Wishbone thought, as he followed the team off the training floor. *I don't really need an MMU. I can perform all those moves with my legs.*

12:00 P.M. After a half hour spent in the museum gift shop, the Charger team gathered in the cafeteria for a quick lunch. Wishbone had been looking forward to an after-meal nap, but there was no time.

The whirlwind of activity continued. The afternoon's schedule included: lectures on Earth ecology and aeronautical engineering, a demo on life inside a space station, a discussion about building a lunar outpost, a quick dinner, and a movie about the flight of the first space shuttle.

The movie was shown in the Spacedome theater, which had a huge curving screen and an awesome sound system. However, Wishbone was a little disappointed that no popcorn was served.

7:00 P.M. Monique, the night counselor, had taken over at three o'clock. She stood before her team on the training floor. The Charger team was about to spend two hours training for their first mission. Before that, however, everyone had to be informed of what their mission assignments would be.

The trainees focused on Monique, many of them seeming a bit jittery. Wishbone gave his side a nervous paw scratch.

"I am going to read out your assignments for both missions," Monique announced. "We have tried to give people the choices they wanted, but that wasn't always possible. And, remember, if you don't get a choice you like on the first mission, you might get something you like better on the second mission. Also, remember this—every single job is very important. Ask anyone who has worked on a real shuttle mission."

She's right. Every job is definitely of great importance. But if I don't get to be pilot . . .

Monique began to read off the assignments.

On the first mission, known as the Alpha Mission, Joe, Sam, and David would all be part of the ground crew. David would be flight director, Joe would be the capcom, and Sam would be the GNC. Wishbone had no idea what these jobs were, but he figured he would find out before long.

Monique smiled at Wishbone. "Sorry, Wishbone, you will just be an observer for this mission."

Wishbone raised his ears in disbelief. *What? Just an observer? I can't afford to take a backseat on this mission. No way. If the counselors didn't think to give me an important job, I'll find one for myself! I need to show everyone what astrodogs can do.*

Monique read the assignments for the second mission, known as the Bravo Mission. For this mission, Joe, Sam, David, and Wishbone would all be part of the flight crew. Sam would be commander, David would be a mission specialist, and Joe would be a pay-load specialist. Wishbone would be assisting Joe with his duties.

Wishbone shifted his ears, very surprised by these assignments. Neither he, Joe, Sam, nor David had been awarded their first choices. The team waited while Monique went away to make some last-minute arrangements.

"What do you guys think of your jobs?" Sam whispered to Joe and David.

"Why did I get payload specialist on the second mission?" Joe said, wrinkling his brow. "That's a science job, and I'm no good at science. You should have gotten that job, David."

David shrugged. "They probably gave it to you because Wishbone is part of the experiments. But why did I get mission specialist on the second mission? I know some of the space-walking involves heights. But heights and I don't get along so well. You should have gotten that, Sam."

"Here's the big question," Sam said, screwing her face into an odd expression. "Why did they make me commander of the Bravo Mission? I don't feel qualified to command a spaceship. That job should have been yours, Joe."

Wishbone was about to growl his own complaints, but then Monique reappeared. Standing alongside Monique were five counselors Wishbone had not yet seen. They would be in charge of preparing the trainees for the two missions.

Okay, no time for griping, Wishbone thought, rising to all fours. *It's time for Joe, Sam, David, and myself to learn our jobs for the Alpha Mission. . . . Oh, yeah, I still don't know what my job is yet.*

I may need a job, but John Ulnar needs a bit of luck. Right now, he's locked away in a pound . . . uh . . . I mean a prison.

75

CHAPTER EIGHT

Back and forth, John paced, back and forth.

John was in a white-walled, brightly lit prison cell, fifty feet below the Purple Palace. Through the duro-glass bars of the cell, John saw a guard walk by. The man was twirling a laser-baton, a weapon used to stun troublesome prisoners.

I hate being locked up, John thought, his nails clicking on the floor as he paced. *Might as well wear a leash, which I also hate. I need to get out of here. For the sake of democracy. For the sake of Aladoree. For the sake of . . . me!*

John sat down to lick the paw that had been zapped by the alien when he tried to stop Eric. After giving John a life sentence in prison, Adam Ulnar had insisted that a doctor treat the wound. John felt much better. It had been only an hour since John's shocking meeting with Supreme Commander Ulnar.

John's ears lifted as he heard a light tapping at his wall. John realized he was being sent a message in the Legion's tapping code. The only prisoners in this wing were the three Legion guards John had wrongly locked up for the murder of Captain Otan. John had gotten to know the men—Jay, Giles, and Samdu—on the brief flight to Phobos, and he liked all three of them.

The message was repeated. John knew it was coming from Jay.

The message said: *John, can you hear me?*

John went to the wall and tapped a return message with his nails.

John's message said: *I hear you. We need to escape. Adam Ulnar is part of the plan to overthrow the Green Government. That's why we've been locked up.*

After a moment, Jay tapped: *Did you say Supreme Commander Adam Ulnar is part of the plan?*

John tapped: *Hard to believe, but true. If we don't escape soon, there is no telling what will happen. Do you have any ideas?*

Jay tapped: *Perhaps one of us could grab the guard's laser-baton.*

John tapped: *Let me try. I'm a bit smaller, so I might have a better chance of surprising him.*

Jay tapped: *Here he comes. Good luck.*

Hearing the guard walk toward his cell, John moved over next to the bars. He called out in a smart-aleck voice, "Hey, Mr. Guard, when do we get some grub around this place? I'm starving!"

The husky guard approached John's cell, twirling his laser-baton. "Wise guy, huh? How would you like—"

In a flash, John shot his muzzle through the bars and grabbed the baton in his teeth. The guard yanked at the baton, but John's strong jaw yanked harder. After pulling the weapon free, John aimed it at the guard and pushed a button.

"Owww!" the guard screamed, as the baton zapped him with a powerful laser beam.

The man fell heavily to the ground. John knew he would be unconscious for about fifteen minutes.

"Excellent!" Jay cried.

John stretched a paw through the bars, toward the fallen guard. He fished in the man's pocket, soon pulling out a collection of keys. In less than a minute, all four men were released from their cells.

Like John, the other three men wore the sky-blue jumpsuits of Legion junior officers. The men no longer wore their guns or supply belts, which had been taken away by the prison guards.

"Nice work," Jay Kalam whispered, as he scratched John between the ears. He was a man from the Africa region of Earth. Jay was slender, handsome, and extremely intelligent. Though still in his early thirties, Jay obviously had the leadership skills that would make him a senior officer one day.

"Thank goodness we're no longer cooped up like a flock of chickens," Giles Habibula said with a wheezing chuckle. He was a man from the England region of Earth. Giles had reddish hair, a bushy moustache, and a potbelly, which clearly showed how much he liked food and drink. The oldest of the group, he looked to be about fifty.

"One of us chickens is fat enough for cooking," Samdu Samdi said, giving Giles a pat on the belly. He was from Titan, one of Saturn's moons. However, his ancestors were originally from the India region of Earth. Samdu was a bald-headed giant of a man, his muscles resembling the mountains of his native moon. He seemed to be in his late thirties.

"Okay, fellas," John whispered, "what do you say we beat it out of here?"

Jay pulled a proton gun from the fallen guard.

Then the four men crept quietly down the hallway, soon stopping at a metal grate that led into the airflow tunnels. Samdu gripped the grate, gritted his teeth, and pulled the grate away with his powerful arms.

The four men climbed through the opening where the grate had been. John was able to get through easily, but for the others it was a tight squeeze. John led the way through the pitch-dark tunnel. Soon the horizontal tunnel turned vertical, and the men climbed a ladder.

"This is miserable work," Giles complained, huffing and puffing. "I feel like we're crawling through the dark insides of a whale. Ochh! It's hot, too!"

"Shh!" Samdu urged. "You'll be even hotter if a proton gun catches you in the backside."

Sideways and up, sideways and up, the four men made their way up through several floors of the Purple Palace. As they traveled, John gave the others the details of his recent meeting with Adam Ulnar.

"Gentlemen, this is a dangerous situation," Jay said with concern. "If Adam Ulnar is part of the plot, that means no one will be notifying Green Hall that the Keeper of AKKA has been kidnapped. The Green Government is at great risk."

John raised his ears, hearing the distant scream of a siren. "Uh-oh. That siren must be meant for us. Before long, every soldier in the building will be chasing after us. We need to hightail it away from Phobos immediately."

"Let's try to catch an elevator to a landing platform," Jay suggested. "Then we may be able to steal a ship."

John led the men to another grate, which Samdu

pulled loose. The men climbed out of the tunnel, hurried down a hallway, then took an elevator to the very top of the Purple Palace.

The elevator let the men off at a landing platform. John could see the lights of Phobos twinkling against the night, two thousand feet below.

Then John saw it, glimmering in the darkness.

On the middle of the platform, a ship lay in a slightly angled horizontal position. It was a torpedo-shaped craft with a central rocket system in its base and three smaller rockets surrounding the hull. The armored shell was glistening silver with blue and red accents. The ship was both powerful and graceful—a perfect flying machine.

"That's the *Purple Dream*," John whispered with awe. "The fastest vessel ever built by mankind. The ship Eric used in his expedition beyond the System."

Samdu released a low whistle. "That is one honey of a ship."

"I believe Supreme Commander Ulnar now uses it as his personal craft," Jay said, eyes glued to the ship. "I had always wondered why Adam called it *Purple Dream*. Now I understand why—because he wants to bring back the Purple Empire!"

Giles scratched at his red hair. "It's not going to be easy breaking into the ship."

John noticed the glow of a nearby red light. "Hey, look, it's the fueling light. That means someone is fueling the ship for use. Probably the Supreme Commander himself."

"Perfect," Jay said, snapping his fingers.

The four men hurried to the side of the ship, hiding so they could not be seen from the elevator. After whispering some strategy ideas, the men waited in silence.

Seconds ticked by. John swished his tail nervously, back and forth, back and forth.

John's tail stopped in mid-swish as an elevator door slid open. Raising his ears, John heard the footsteps of eight people.

Though John couldn't see the people, he picked out the voice of Adam Ulnar. "I'm sure they'll catch those escaped rascals any minute now. I'd like to wait, but if I'm late for this meeting on Io, too many questions will be asked."

John heard the high-pitched beeps of a compu-key. This was followed by the near-silent sound of the hatch popping open. John made a signal with his paw.

The escaped men set their plan in motion.

As Samdu lifted Jay high enough to see over the ship's side, Jay fired three quick shots with his stolen proton gun. Three zings of the gun were followed by three grunts. Immediately, the four escaped men rushed from their hiding place.

John saw the stunned faces of the white-bearded Adam Ulnar and seven soldiers. Three of the soldiers lay wounded on the ground.

"Capture them!" Adam ordered his men.

As planned, John raced straight for Adam. His job was to make sure the Supreme Commander didn't get away. He seized the man's pants leg in his teeth, holding on for dear life.

This move isn't exactly in the academy manual, but it's highly effective.

By now, the enemy soldiers had whipped out their own proton guns. Giles had also taken a fallen soldier's gun. The mighty Samdu used only his bare hands.

Thin beams of violet light zinged from the guns. All

was confusion—yelling fighters, sizzling pistols, zapped metal, crazy patterns of violet light. Still grasping Adam's leg, John felt the deadly force of a beam whiz over his head.

"Let go of me!" Adam raged, shaking his ankle furiously.

One of Adam's men darted onto the *Purple Dream* and began to close the hatch. Samdu scrambled up the ladder in time to stop the hatch with his fist. The giant from Titan tossed the man out as if he were a sack of potatoes.

In a matter of seconds, the fight was over.

Using the element of surprise, the escaped prisoners had proven victorious. Every one of Adam's soldiers was either wounded or weaponless.

"Come!" Samdu called from the hatchway.

As Samdu kept the enemy back with a gun, Jay and Giles hurried up the ladder. When John dragged Adam to the ladder, Jay and Giles each grabbed one of the Supreme Commander's arms. They yanked Adam upward, with John still clinging doggedly to the ankle of Adam's pants.

When all five men were inside, Giles closed the hatch and locked it shut. As John finally released Adam, Samdu wrapped a muscular arm around the man's waist.

"Not so hard, you brute!" Adam cried.

Samdu squeezed the man even tighter.

"First things first," Jay told his companions. "Let's get out of here."

"The ship's not done fueling," Giles said, glancing at a red light. "If we're going on a long trip, we don't want to be caught short."

"We can't afford to wait," Jay advised. "Any

second now they'll be firing a missile at us from the next landing platform. They'll probably use a radiation missile so they can rescue and treat the Supreme Commander before he dies. We need to launch at once."

"I can do it!" John said, already trotting away.

John hurried through the ship's main cabin and then entered the flight deck. It was a small chamber with four seats. A view shield curved around the entire area. John had never seen this model of ship, so he wasn't sure what all the dials, buttons, switches, lights, and screens on the control panel were for. But that didn't matter, because a collection of flickering lights indicated the ship's computer was turned on. What John didn't know, the computer would.

John jumped into the pilot's chair. "What is your name?" he asked the computer.

The computer replied in a whispery female voice. "My name is Sal. Will you be the pilot of this flight?"

"Yes, Sal," John told the computer. "Are we prepared to launch?"

"All systems are go," the computer replied. "Except the fuel supply is only eighteen-point-seven

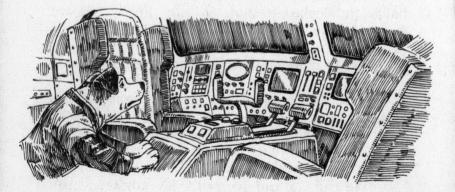

percent full. To complete fueling it will take twelve minutes, fifteen sec——"

"We don't have time. Stop the fueling."

"Roger," the computer said, as the red fueling light turned off. John knew Sal wasn't calling him "Roger." That was the term used to say that someone or something understood a request.

Jay and Giles entered the flight deck, where both men took seats. "Samdu's holding Adam back in the main cabin," Jay told John. "I'm quite sure they'll be firing a missile at us any second, so we need to get moving."

John bent back his ears, something he often did while flying.

"Go to vertical," John told the computer. "Quickly."

"Roger," the computer replied.

Automatically, seat-straps crisscrossed the chest of each passenger. In a swift but smooth movement, the entire ship tilted from a horizontal to a vertical position. John and the others were flipped onto their backs.

"Begin liftoff," John told the computer.

"The missile will come any moment!" Giles cried in panic. "Sure as Mercury gets hot!"

"Come on, come on," Jay whispered tensely.

"Pilot, what is our destination?" the computer asked.

"I'm not sure yet," John said hurriedly. "Right now, just carry us away from Phobos as fast as possible."

"Roger," the computer replied. "Ten . . . nine . . . eight . . . sev——"

"Now!" John barked.

John felt the tremendous takeoff blast beneath

his tail. The chair's cushioning pressed firmly against John's back. Flaming rockets were shooting the ship upward with thousands of pounds of explosive force.

"Here we go!" John cried with relief. "Off into the wild black yonder!"

CHAPTER NINE

Through the view shield, John watched the blue sky quickly darken into the blackness of space. The seat-straps opened automatically. The prisoners on the *Purple Dream* had made a successful escape from Phobos.

"Great work, kid!" Jay said, giving John's head a pat.

"Perhaps we should contact Green Hall," Giles suggested. "They need to know about Adam's plan to overthrow the government."

"It's too risky," Jay said. "The message might get intercepted, which would make it easier for our enemies to find us."

"Have we decided on a destination?" Sal, the computer, asked in its whispery female voice.

"Not yet," Jay answered. "For now, Sal, maintain our present course and speed. John, Giles, let's go talk to Adam Ulnar. We need a few more details before we know where we're going."

John, Jay, and Giles left the flight deck. They entered the main cabin, which was the largest room on the ship. It contained travel seats, a lounge area, exercise area, and dining area. Adam sat across the dining table from Samdu, who kept a proton gun handy. Jay, Giles, and John took seats.

"We need some information," Jay told Adam in a businesslike manner. "Earlier in the day, you told John that the Medusas took Eric and Aladoree to their home planet. Would that be a planet that revolves around the star Alpha Centauri? Supposedly, that is the only planet Eric visited on his famous expedition."

"That is correct," Adam answered. "They have gone to the solar system of Alpha Centauri."

John took a deep sniff with his little black nose. He could smell Adam's nervousness level increase.

"He's lying," John told his companions. "Trust me, I have a nose for this sort of thing."

Samdu aimed the gun at Adam, as if he was about to shoot.

"All right," Adam said, a drop of sweat trickling down his forehead. "I was lying. Do not shoot me."

Giles leaned forward. "Then, for the sake of your good health, tell us where Eric and Aladoree have gone."

Adam raised both hands. "I'll tell you, honestly. Eric did go to a planet in Alpha Centauri's solar system on his expedition. But when he found no life on the planet, he decided to visit the solar system of a second star. Barnard's Star. That is the star the Medusas' planet revolves around. And that is where the Medusas have taken Eric and Aladoree."

"We must go there," John said quietly. "We need to rescue Aladoree before she is killed or forced to give away the secret of AKKA. Otherwise, Eric and the Medusas might really take over the Green Government. What's more, we've got the only ship in the System capable of making this journey."

"I agree with John," Jay said with a serious nod. "But I'd like us all to agree on this. Giles? Samdu?"

Giles slapped the table. "By the sword of my ancestors, I say we go!"

"I say we go, too," Samdu said simply.

"Fools," Adam said with a mocking sneer. "You don't have nearly enough fuel to make it to Barnard's Star. And even if you did, you would never survive once you got there. The Medusas' planet contains dangers beyond your worst nightmares. The best thing you can do is give up at once!"

Jay looked at Samdu. "Lock him in one of the cabins. We will need more information from him at a later date. Make sure he cannot get to the weapons and has no means of escape."

Samdu took Adam to the rear of the ship, keeping the gun at the Supreme Commander's back.

Jay began pacing the cabin as he thought. "This

won't be easy. Barnard's Star is the second closest star to our Solar System. But that doesn't mean it's close."

"Aye, far from it," Giles added. "So far, it's about six light-years away."

John looked out a porthole, where he saw the stars glimmering against the blackness. The stars were so great in number that they almost seemed to be countless fragments from a shattered crystal vase.

John knew the stars were so far away that their distances were measured in light-years. That was the distance a beam of light traveled in a single year— almost six trillion miles. If a star was one hundred light-years away, that meant you were able to see the star only as it appeared one hundred years ago. The stars were so incredibly distant that they appeared as tiny specks of white. However, they were really gigantic, sun-sized bodies of yellow, red, or blue.

John asked the computer a question, knowing it was listening in all parts of the ship. "Sal, how quickly can we reach Barnard's Star?"

Sal gave a quick answer, even though the question involved very complicated mathematical calculations. "The maximum speed of this ship is one hundred fifty times the speed of light. Traveling at max speed most of the way, we can reach Barnard's Star in approximately two weeks."

Giles raised a finger. "Aye, that's all well and good. But our fuel tank is only eighteen percent full. Barely enough to get us near Uranus at a decent speed. Certainly not all the way to Barnard's star and back."

Samdu, who had rejoined the group, threw in his opinion. "And this ship uses pymel fuel. It'll be very tough to come by, because only a handful of ships use it. They probably have some pymel on Phobos. And then there's plenty on Pluto, where the stuff is mined and manufactured."

Jay snapped his fingers. "Pluto—yes! We'll pick up more pymel on Pluto."

"Zounds, man!" Giles said, slapping his forehead. "Have you not heard a word I've said? Pluto's farther than Uranus. A few billion miles farther! We can't make it there at a decent speed!"

John raised a paw. "We can make it there at a decent speed if we swing around Jupiter, using a slingshot effect. I did it many times during my training. The slingshot will give us a big speed boost without using up any extra fuel."

"Aye, lad," Giles said excitedly. "That should work. How we get the fuel on Pluto—now, that's another matter."

"We'll cross that icy bridge when we come to it," Jay joked.

Suddenly, the group heard Adam pounding on the locked door of his cabin, shouting with rage. "Fools, you will be beaten! Give up while you still have the chance!"

"Ignore him," Jay told the men. "Right now, we need to get organized. Divide up assignments."

John jumped out of his chair and nudged Jay's leg with his muzzle. "The choice for commander is obvious. Jay has the coolest head and the best mind. Do the rest of you agree?"

"Definitely," Giles and Samdu said together.

"Very well," Jay said with a polite nod. "I shall be our commander. Giles, in your youth you were a flight engineer. Do you think you're capable of handling this ship's engine room? It'll be a bit different from what you're used to."

Giles waved a hand. "Pooh, engines are engines. And I'll be the chef, as well. I'm very skilled with food, both preparing and eating."

"Yeah, when do we eat?" John asked, licking his chops.

"Soon," Giles said, patting his potbelly.

"No, later," Jay said, already acting the boss. "Samdu, you'll be in charge of defense. If we need to use the ship's cannons or missiles, you're the one who will operate them. I believe those weapons are even more powerful than your fists."

"Aye, aye, sir," Samdu said with a salute.

Jay knelt down to John. "How good a pilot are you?"

"I don't like to brag, sir," John said, looking modestly at his paws. "But I'm about as good as it gets."

"Then you shall be our pilot," Jay stated.

"Yippeee!" John yelled, running and leaping into the air. Realizing this was not appropriate behavior, he calmed down and said, "I mean yes, sir. It will be my privilege."

Jay held out a fist and said, "Legion bond."

This was an unofficial gesture among Legion soldiers, to show their unity. Giles placed a fist on top of Jay's, Samdu placed a fist on top of Giles's, and John placed a paw at the top.

"Legion of Space!" all four of the men shouted together.

"Now, John, go fly this ship!" Jay ordered.

John trotted into the flight deck and jumped into the pilot's seat. He spoke to the computer. "Sal, my gal, we've decided on a destination. Pluto. And to get us there on our low fuel supply, we will first slingshot around Jupiter. Give me the fastest possible speed without using up our fuel."

"Roger," Sal replied, instantly adjusting the ship's course.

John watched the digits on the speed meter race by, finally settling at one-fifth XL.

John didn't feel much difference, but the *Purple Dream* was now accelerating to one-fifth the speed of light. John knew that was two hundred thousand times the speed of sound, or one hundred thirty-four million miles per hour.

John placed a paw on a rectangular box where some of Sal's circuits were housed. "Allow me to say, Sal, that I think you are one excellent computer."

"Thank you, pilot."

"Uh . . . listen, why don't you call me 'John'?"

"Yes, John."

John was very glad to have Sal aboard. He was well aware the computer knew more about the ship's inner workings than any human ever could. Indeed, computers had grown very sophisticated since their birth in the twentieth century. In the twenty-fifth century, computers grew so complex that they began to take on human thoughts and feelings.

Soon after, they also took on human shape.

Computerized brains were placed inside artificial but lifelike bodies. This process formed a type of creature known as an "android." It was often difficult telling androids apart from humans.

The Purple Empire made great use of androids in its royal armies. When the Green Government came to power, however, it began to outlaw any type of computer with human thoughts and feelings. The government considered the use of these computers a type of slavery. It also feared the computers might one day rise up against their human masters.

Nowadays, computers were just machines. Yet each one had a different name and voice, and they often seemed very human indeed.

"John," Sal said in its whispery female voice, "you may wish to know that we are entering the Asteroid Belt."

A moment later, John heard rocks pelting the ship's armored shell. It sounded like hail hammering a rooftop. John knew the Asteroid Belt was a circle of swirling rock-metal fragments that covered most of the distance between Mars and Jupiter. Some of the asteroids were as small as dog biscuits, while others were as large as Alaska.

"Sal, you'd better give me manual control," John said, as he placed his paw on a joystick.

"Roger," Sal replied.

Manual control meant the pilot controlled the ship's movements. This was useful when the pilot's instincts and vision were needed for certain maneuvers. At other times, Sal could control the ship's movements with autopilot.

John spent the next hundred million miles steering away from the most dangerous asteroids. Sal, of course, was a big help.

About three hours after leaving Mars, Jupiter came into view. By far the largest body in the System, Jupiter was bigger than a thousand Earths put together. The planet looked like a magnificent marble, its surface rippling with countless shades of red, orange, yellow, brown, and white.

John bent back his ears, knowing it was time for the slingshot effect. John shook out his paw, then gripped the joystick.

The brilliantly colored Jupiter drew closer, until nothing else could be seen through the view shield. When the planet was only two million miles away, John began to make a wide circle that followed the planet's curving surface.

Easy, easy, John thought, as he worked the joystick. *Remember, keep a light touch, John.*

Though he didn't feel it, John knew the ship was gradually gathering the force of Jupiter's gravity. After a minute or so, the *Purple Dream* had traveled just over halfway around the planet.

Now!

As John angled the joystick, the *Purple Dream* shot straight away from Jupiter's curve—like a pebble flung from a slingshot.

"Nicely done, John," Sal said. "We have increased our speed by thirty-three million miles an hour. We should reach Pluto in approximately nineteen hours."

"Here we come, Pluto," John said, his tail wagging with satisfaction. "Boy, do I love flying! It makes me hungry, though. Sal, you wouldn't happen to have anything to eat, would you?"

The Legion Academy seems to have trained John well. Let's see how the training is going for my friends—Sam, David, and Joe—and me back at the Space Academy.

Chapter Ten

Tuesday morning, Susan, the day counselor, led the Charger team outside into Rocket Park. The collection of proudly towering rockets shone brightly in the sun, all the more so because most of them were painted white.

Wishbone felt well rested and ready for another day at Space Academy. The night before, the training session for the Alpha Mission had gone quite well. The team had spent two hours training and another hour reviewing. Then everyone had gone to bed, exhausted.

"It's not easy getting a vehicle up into space," Susan told the team. "Why is that?"

"Gravity!" almost everyone called out.

"Yes," Susan said with a big nod. "That's where rockets come into the picture. Rockets create explosions that literally shove the vehicle beyond gravity's pull. Those capsules we saw in the museum yesterday were all shot into space by rockets."

Susan took the team from rocket to rocket, giving them all sorts of information on the growth and advances of rocketry. As the tour progressed, the rockets grew larger.

Finally, the team came to the largest rocket of all. This one lay stretched on the ground like a sleeping giant, longer than a football field. It was divided into three sections, or stages. At the end of the last stage lay the capsule that was designed to carry astronauts.

Susan gestured at the huge rocket. "Folks, this is the *Saturn Five*—the biggest, longest, most powerful rocket ever built. It carries about three thousand tons of fuel. This is the type of rocket that sent the *Apollo* astronauts all the way to the moon."

Wishbone stared with awe at the mighty *Saturn Five* rocket. *What was it Neil Armstrong said back in 1969, just as he took the first human step on the moon? Oh, yes, I remember: "That's one small step for man, one giant leap for all mankind." I couldn't have said it better myself, Neil.*

9:30 A.M. Susan led the team to a series of small barrackslike structures not far from the Habitat. Inside one of these structures, the team gathered in a school-like room with chairs and long tables.

"Now we're going to build our own rockets," Susan said as she passed out little boxes. "These rockets will work very much like the ones we just saw. They just won't be quite as big."

Wishbone sat perched on a chair between Joe and David. He watched Joe pull out the contents of his box—flat pieces of wood, cardboard tubes, a light-weight cone, a sheet of plastic, string, and a few other items. In addition, each trainee was given a pair of scissors, glue, and a pencil.

The team began to build their rockets. Susan would describe a step in the construction process, and then all the students would follow it.

The rocket-building was a breeze for David, who had constructed far more complex machines in his garage laboratory. Other trainees ran into problems, though, because the work required precise measure-ments and careful assembling.

Joe had a tough time with things of a scientific nature. Among other problems, he couldn't get the wooden fins to stay on the bottom stage of his rocket.

David leaned over to help. "You can't use too much glue or it gets gloppy. A thin line of glue is just enough."

Joe discovered that he had accidentally glued his plastic parachute to his hand. "Isn't it funny that I'm the scientist on the Bravo Mission? That should make things real interesting."

"Don't worry, Joe. I have complete confidence that you'll do a fine job," Wishbone said, as he pawed at a piece of spare cardboard. "I'll help you turn into a rocket scientist."

12:30 P.M. After a lecture on daily life in the space shuttle and then lunch, Susan took the team for a second visit to the Space & Rocket Center museum.

This time, the trainees got to experience two fantastic rides that were in the museum, open to the general public. On the ride called Mars Mission, the trainees entered a dark chamber, where they rode a wild roller coaster across the surface of Mars. On Journey to Jupiter, the trainees entered a dark chamber, where they zipped past the speed of light on a kaleidoscopic trip to Jupiter.

Then the trainees were allowed some time to roam the museum on their own. The museum contained lots of interactive exhibits, and Wishbone and his friends spent some time playing a really interesting video game. The object of the game was to land a vehicle on the moon, while controlling the vehicle's movement and fuel output.

As Sam pushed buttons, she closely watched a screen that showed a graphic of the lowering vehicle. "I can't seem to keep it away from this mountain," Sam called out.

"Use the fuel thruster," Joe advised. "And try to keep a lighter touch on the controls."

Sam tried to take the advice, but the vehicle crashed into the mountain anyway. A terrible explosion was followed by the message: "The lunar module has crashed. No survivors."

Sam tried several more landings, each one ending in disaster.

Sam stared at the frustrating game. "Why did they make me commander for the Bravo Mission? I'll have everyone's lives in my hands, and obviously I'm not ready to fly a spaceship."

"Oh, you'll get the hang of it," Wishbone said, giving Sam a reassuring nudge. "At least I hope you do. Because I'll be a passenger on your flight!"

3:00 P.M. After some free time for basketball and four-square, Monique, the night counselor, took over for Susan. She took the team onto the training floor, where she stood beside another strange device. This one looked much like the manned maneuvering unit, except the chair was smaller and there were no armrests with controls.

"This simulator is called the five-degree-of-freedom chair," Monique told the team. "It's also known as the Five DF. It will show you what it would be like to do a space-walk, or EVA, while attached only to a long cord. Unlike the MMU, the Five DF has no controls. You just float free. As you'll discover, the only way you can do anything is by grabbing onto something with your hands or feet."

One by one, the trainees tried out the 5DF chair. As the chair moved this way and that on a motorized cushion of air, the trainees swerved and swung about. They could, however, control their movements by grabbing onto yellow bars that were attached to a nearby structure.

When Wishbone trotted over to the five-degree-of-freedom chair, Monique allowed him to have a go at it. But the dog ran into trouble because he couldn't reach the yellow bars with his paws. All he could do was float helplessly in place.

Seeing the dog grow frustrated, Monique quickly took Wishbone out of the chair.

Whoops, Wishbone thought, as Monique set him gently on the floor. *I didn't do so great on that one. I hope this doesn't count against me too much.*

Wishbone noticed a group of visitors watching the trainees from behind a railing.

Of course! Why didn't I think of it before? NASA must have someone here on the grounds watching me. Checking me out. Seeing whether or not I've got the right stuff to be an astrodog. Okay, from now on I need to operate at peak performance level at all times—for the sake of dogs everywhere.

The rest of the day stayed busy. The team watched a movie about exploring planets, and they heard a lecture on spinoffs, which were products developed for space travel that were also very useful on Earth. The team also observed some scuba divers working in a big underwater tank. They were demonstrating how astronauts trained for working in the weightless conditions of space-walks.

For the rest of the day, however, Wishbone felt quite certain that someone from NASA was keeping a careful eye on him.

CHAPTER ELEVEN

That evening, the Alpha Mission began. This would be the first of the Charger team's two missions into space.

Wishbone glanced around at the alert faces of the six other trainees who would be working with him on the ground crew. They sat in the mission operations control room, a darkened room just off the training floor.

In the room there were two rows, each containing work stations with computer screens and a variety of lights, switches, and buttons. Wishbone was perched in a swivel chair at the end of the back row, right between Joe and David.

All of the trainees, except Wishbone, wore a headset with a microphone. The trainees spoke into their mikes, even though they were usually speaking to someone in the same room. Wishbone's hearing was so sharp that he had no need for a headset.

Wishbone heard a chorus of serious voices.

"Booster-prop?"

"Go."

"Mission scientist?"

"Go."

"Capcom?"

"I'm a go."

"Ground audio check is complete."

This is so cool, Wishbone thought, his tail thumping with excitement. *It may not be the real thing, but it sure feels like it.*

The ten other trainees on the team were on the training floor. Seven would be going on a simulated flight in the shuttle. Three others would be working in a model of a space station.

At the front of the room, a big screen showed the *Discovery,* a real space shuttle that had flown many missions. It stood vertically on the NASA launch pad in Florida, waiting for liftoff. The screen would be showing a videotaped flight of an actual shuttle mission. However, everything would be controlled by an "unseen" counselor in a nearby booth. He would make sure that the shuttle's movements worked in relation to the Charger team's mission.

The ground crew would monitor every single aspect of the shuttle flight—by operating controls, checking lists, giving advice, keeping things on schedule, and, most important, making sure the shuttle and its crew returned safely to Earth. This was the way it was on real shuttle missions, except on the real missions there were more than fifty people at a time working in the control room.

"Everybody, you're doing great," Wishbone whispered to his fellow members of the ground crew. "Paws up!"

He noticed Sam sending a friendly smile his way.

Time for a time check.

Television monitors at the left and right of the

room showed the mission time. Both monitors showed the same message in green letters: T–9:00 and holding.

The "T" referred to liftoff time. The minus sign indicated how much time was left before liftoff. Later, a plus sign would indicate how much time had passed since the liftoff. The clock always "held" for a while at nine minutes to allow extra time for preparation.

"Commander," Joe said into his mike, "if you don't mind, it's time to close those cabin vents."

Joe's position was capcom, the person in charge of communicating with the flight crew. Most of the time, the capcom's mike was the only one that fed into *Discovery*. In real life, the capcom was always an astronaut, because he or she would know just what the astronauts in flight were experiencing. Joe's confident but friendly manner was just right for the job.

David sat on the other side of Wishbone. The boy moved his eyes around the room, watching every person and screen like a hawk.

His position was flight director, which meant he oversaw and coordinated every aspect of the *Discovery* mission. He was the boss of the ground crew, and he was really the boss of the flight crew, too. David's ability to focus on doing many complex tasks at once made him perfect for the job.

After checking some figures on her computer screen, Sam spoke into her mike. "Okay, folks, time to start the count. Let's go to T minus nine minutes and counting."

Sam sat across an aisle at the next bank in the back row. She was the GNC, or guidance, navigational, and control officer. Sam had many different responsibilities, which she handled with her usual intelligence and enthusiasm.

Wishbone watched the two time screens come to life. They now showed: T–8:59. As the trainees continued to talk into their mikes and flip switches, the seconds ticked away.

Wishbone gave his side a nervous scratch. *I'm sure there's a camera hidden somewhere in this room so whoever NASA has sent to watch me can keep an eye on my performance. They need to see if I'm ready for the astrodog program. The counselors didn't give me a job on this mission, but I've taken care of that myself. I've given myself perhaps the most important job here—MWD. Also known as Mission Watchdog.*

"Flight director," Joe said evenly, "commander tells me the course bearing ninety-point-zero is entered into the onboard computers."

"Roger on that," David replied, as he flipped several switches at his bank.

Each trainee had a script in front of him or her. The script told every person what to do and say, and exactly what time to do or say it. Though it was similar to the script of a play, not everything was prearranged.

The trainees had to use their own wording and complete often complicated assignments in small amounts of time. And sometimes unexpected problems would arise, which the trainees had to figure out how to solve. Even though this exercise was "just pretend," there was no guarantee everything would come out A-okay.

That's where my job comes into the picture.

Wishbone focused his eyes on a TV screen that showed the commander and pilot in a mock-up of *Discovery's* flight deck. Right between the two astronauts lay the "caution and warning" screen. If a red light appeared on this screen, that signaled a mechanical malfunction, which in plain English meant "big technical problem." In the training session the day before, the trainees had been so busy with their different tasks that they had been slow to spot the malfunctions.

Slowness can be deadly. So the second I spot a red light, I'll inform David of the problem. That's why I'm called the Mission Watchdog.

At T–5:15, David said, "Capcom, tell *Discovery* they may begin full start of auxiliary power units."

"Pilot," Joe said, "why don't you start those APUs?"

"Roger," the pilot replied.

On the big screen, billows of smoke began to rise from the base of *Discovery*. As soon as the smoke appeared, Wishbone felt the tension in the room go up several notches. He realized his tail was flicking back and forth with concern.

The preparations continued in a professional manner. However, at one point, Wishbone heard a mumbling voice.

"Who is that mumbling?" David asked, a bit irritated.

Wishbone knew it was Ryan, a skinny boy who sat two seats down the row. He always wore a big base-ball cap that seemed to swallow his head.

"It was me, the booster-and-propulsion guy," Ryan confessed. "I said the oh-two valves are closing."

"Thank you," David said. "I didn't mean to get annoyed with you, booster-prop, but it's important we all speak clearly."

"Roger," Ryan said.

Soon the INCO, or instrument, navigation, and communications officer, who sat in the front row, began counting. "Twelve . . . eleven . . . ten . . . nine . . . eight . . . seven . . ."

Wishbone jumped, hearing a distant rumbling. On the big screen, great puffs of smoke began to shoot out from underneath the shuttle.

"We have main engine start," the booster-prop said.

The INCO kept counting. "four . . . three . . . two . . . one . . . zero . . ."

"We have SRB ignition and liftoff!" the booster-prop announced.

Wishbone heard the distant boom of an explosion. A mountain of orange-yellow-white smoke surrounded the shuttle, floating across the entire screen. Birds were seen scattering wildly. And . . . *Discovery* shot straight upward.

Everyone watched tensely. Wishbone knew the most dangerous stages of the mission were the liftoff and landing. One of the real shuttles, *Challenger,* had exploded only seconds after its liftoff, killing all its crew. That was only the second time in NASA's forty-year history that astronaut lives had been lost during a flight.

As the shuttle continued to rise, Sam announced, "*Discovery* has cleared the tower. A perfect liftoff. Houston, we're turning things over to you."

Wishbone knew that in real life there were actually three mission operations control rooms. Cape Canaveral, Florida, supervised the liftoff. The one in Houston, Texas, oversaw the flight. The one in Huntsville, Alabama, ran the scientific experiments. At Space Academy, however, everything was done in a single control room.

The view on the big screen had shifted upward. Now Wishbone could see *Discovery* sailing higher and higher into a blue sky. A continuous stream of flame and smoke shot out of the rockets.

At T+2:00, the two long white rockets were ejected. These were the SRBs, or solid rocket boosters, which were responsible for sending the ship halfway up to space. Once their job was done, they would fall into the Atlantic Ocean, where they would be picked up and used on another mission.

So far, so good. What's the time? Are we keeping on schedule here?

As the seconds ticked by, ground and flight crews worked together, performing a variety of complex tasks. Soon *Discovery* could be seen only as a tiny flaming ball.

Even as Wishbone watched the big screen, he kept a close watch on the TV screen that showed the flight deck's "caution-and-warning" screen.

At T+8:45, the jumbo dark orange rocket was ejected. This was the ET, or external tank, which was responsible for sending the ship the rest of the way into space. The rocket would burn away into nothing as it fell through Earth's atmosphere.

Now *Orbiter,* the airplanelike part of the shuttle, was on its own. This was the part of the ship that carried the flight crew.

"Commander," Joe said, "execute OMS burn at ten-oh-five."

The OMS, or orbital maneuvering system, was made up of engines that would send *Orbiter* into orbit around Earth. This meant *Orbiter* would circle Earth in space, kept on a steady path by Earth's gravitational pull.

Merissa, a girl in the front row who always wore a hockey jersey, spoke into her mike. "Payload specialists, this is your ground-crew mission scientist. As soon as the OMS burn is complete, you may start powering up the space lab."

"When will the OMS burn be complete?" a confused scientist on the shuttle asked.

"Uh . . . I'm not sure," Merissa replied. "I think the commander will tell . . . no, wait, the flight director will . . . uh . . . let me find out."

At T+12:00, *Orbiter* entered its Earth orbit, two hundred miles above the ground. The big screen showed the view as seen by a camera on *Orbiter.* Against the blackness of space, the upper third of the globe was visible. From that height, Earth looked much like a multicolored ball.

"Isn't that something?" Wishbone whispered to Joe. "One minute the ship's sitting on the ground. A few minutes later, the thing is in space!"

The pace in the control room slowed down a bit, and a few people even stood up for a stretch.

Wishbone got a chance to deal with an itch that had been bothering him. Actual shuttle missions lasted more than a week, but this one would last only an hour and thirty-five minutes.

As the minutes ticked by, the ground crew worked at various assignments—making sure the ship stayed in sound shape, releasing a satellite that would help read weather conditions, supervising the scientific experiments and space-walking, and docking with the space station.

At one point, Wishbone heard a strange request. "Flight director, this is INCO. Can I go to the bathroom?"

"Uh, I guess so," David replied. "If you don't have anything really important coming up."

The INCO, or instrument, navigation, and communications officer, a cocky boy named Sean, went bolting out of the control room.

Moments later, Wishbone jumped to attention. He saw one of the red lights appear on the flight deck's "caution-and-warning" screen. This meant there was a mechanical problem on *Discovery*. Neither commander nor pilot spotted the light.

Before Wishbone could say anything, David spotted the light himself.

"Okay, we've got a malfunction," David said, just a little nervously.

Come on, come on, come on. Fix the problem. Lives are at stake here!

At David's request, Joe informed the commander of the problem. Then the commander checked his screen to see exactly what the problem was. After the commander identified the problem, he and David began to look through their lists of malfunction solutions. This was because some of the solutions were in the flight director's manual, and some were in the commander's manual.

Uh-oh!

At that point, Wishbone spotted a second red light. David was so busy studying his manual, he didn't notice that one. Neither did anyone else.

Wishbone turned to David. "Flight director, this is MWD, Mission Watchdog. I'm afraid we've got another problem."

David didn't seem to hear.

"Flight director," Wishbone said more loudly. "I repeat. We are showing a *second* problem. And we all know that two problems add up to a crisis!"

David turned a page in his manual.

Why is it no one ever listens to the dog? Not even during a state of emergency!

Wishbone gave a sharp bark.

"Shh!" David said, as he reached over to give Wishbone a pat.

As David did this, his eyes drifted up to the screen showing the flight deck. David sprang to his feet with a look of alarm.

"Hey, we've got another problem here!" David told Joe, his nervousness doubling. "Tell *Discovery* they have the solution for the first malfunction. But they are also showing a second malfunction."

As capcom, Joe spoke in a calm and controlled voice. "Commander, flight director tells me you've got the fix on that first malfunction in your manual. Don't rush yourself. But as soon as you get the problem fixed, we want you to identify a second malfunction that is showing on your caution-warning screen."

Good job, Joe.

The capcom's voice was the only one heard by the flight crew for two reasons. First, it kept things simpler for the flight crew to hear only one voice. Second, the capcom could keep his voice calm, no matter how frantic things were becoming in the control room.

After fixing the first problem, the commander told Joe the nature of the second problem. Joe passed the information on to David, who found the proper solution in his manual. Through Joe, David told the commander exactly how to fix the second problem.

Then all was well.

Whew, things really got tense for a few seconds. But everything got fixed in time, thanks to some great teamwork. Good thing there was a Mission Watchdog for this mission.

At T+1:10:00, it was time to start the complicated business of getting *Discovery* back on the ground. *Orbiter* positioned itself for reentry, the orbital-maneuvering-system engines nudged it toward Earth, and then gravity pulled it back into Earth's atmosphere.

Soon the big screen showed the shuttle soaring through the sky like an airplane. It zoomed to a nice landing on an extra-long runway in Florida, where it would soon be ready for yet another journey into space.

"*Discovery*, welcome home," Joe told the flight crew, wearing a big smile. "Congratulations on a terrific mission!"

Everyone in the room broke into a loud round of applause. Wishbone ran to the door and waited for someone to open it. He wanted to be the first one to give the *Discovery* crew members a congratulatory lick on the face.

Discovery just landed on Earth, and *Purple Dream* is about to land on Pluto. Dress warm. I hear it's pretty darned cold out there.

CHAPTER TWELVE

With rocket flames flaring out of its tail, *Purple Dream* landed on the planet Pluto.

As promised by Sal, the journey from Phobos to Pluto had taken only about nineteen hours. Indeed, it had been only a single day since Aladoree had been kidnapped on Mars. But so much had happened since then, it seemed like ages ago to John.

"Pluto," John said as he jumped off his pilot seat. "Last stop in our Solar System."

Minutes later, John, Jay, and Giles climbed down the ship's ladder. Each man was wearing a special atmo-suit with a bubble helmet. The conditions on Pluto were so harsh that every single part of the body needed protection. Samdu stayed aboard *Purple Dream* to guard the ship and the prisoner, Adam Ulnar.

Once John had his four paws on Pluto's surface, he took a look around. The place didn't look very inviting. The ground was nothing but purplish-gray ice, with puffs of vapor drifting upward. John checked the temperature reading on his watch, which showed –2,011 degrees.

John's atmo-suit was heated, and giant heat lamps with glowing red reflectors were placed around the area on tall stands. Even so, he felt the cold biting sharply through his suit, deep into his fur.

"*Brrr!*" John muttered. "I'm freezing my tail off."

"'*Brrr!*' is right," Giles agreed. "Here we are, shivering on the ice like a herd of lost polar bears!"

No real terra-forming was possible on Pluto. It was too cold. This was because Pluto lay more than three billion miles away from the sun, the source of warmth in the System. There was only one kind of day on this planet—a cold, lonely, frozen, dark night.

Up ahead stood a complex of buildings painted bright orange. This was the base camp for Extar, a company that mined and manufactured the type of fuel known as pymel. Pymel was made from a rare substance found only beneath Pluto's icy surface. It was the only fuel that could propel a ship at speeds high enough to reach the stars.

A figure in an atmo-suit stepped out of a building. He approached the men by hopping great distances across the purplish-gray ground. Pluto had very little gravity, and the atmo-suits added only a small degree of artificial weight.

The man stopped a few feet away from the Legion soldiers. He was a middle-aged fellow with a scraggly beard and bloodshot eyes.

The man spoke gruffly through his helmet mike. "Ahoy! They call me Pappy Nana. I'm in charge of this camp. Who the heck are you?"

"We are soldiers of the Legion of Space," Jay said, speaking into his helmet mike. "We are on a top-secret emergency mission. Supreme Commander Adam Ulnar told us to stop here for pymel fuel and supplies.

He couldn't give you advance notice because he feared someone might listen in on his communication channels."

Nana laughed, showing a set of yellowed teeth. "I don't believe you scalawags. If the Supreme Commander had wanted me to give you fuel and supplies, he would have told me so. I think you've *stolen* that fine ship. Yes, sirree, I think you boys are *pirates!*"

John's sharp ears picked up a whirring noise. He turned to see a proton cannon slip through an opening in the *Purple Dream.*

Zzzzzttt!

A powerful beam of violet light sprang from the cannon's mouth. Big chunks of ice flew into the air. Obviously, Samdu was listening to the conversation and decided Pappy Nana needed to see a show of force.

"What's the big idea!" Nana yelled, whipping out a proton gun.

Jay whipped out a gun equally fast. The two men faced off, aiming their weapons at each other.

Jay spoke with determination. "Yes, Mr. Nana, we are pirates. And we have indeed stolen that ship. But we did it for a good cause. I can't explain all the details. But if we don't get pymel fuel immediately, the Green Government will be in a state of extreme danger. I beg of you, sir, to trust us on this matter. We need that fuel!"

"And food," Giles added. "Lots of food."

"Yes, lots of food," John agreed.

A ferocious gust of wind blew by, almost knocking John off his paws.

Nana looked at the three men, studying their faces. "Call me crazy, but I think you fellas are telling the truth. Lay off with the cannon, and I'll fill you up with all the pymel you can carry. Supplies, too."

"Thank you," Jay said, as both men lowered their guns.

Pappy Nana made a friendly gesture. "Now, why don't you three come inside? While my workers load your ship, I'll treat you to the best hot chocolate in this galaxy."

Traveling by long hops, the men made their way to the complex of orange buildings. Nana took the men to his office, a messy but well-heated room. As John, Jay, and Giles removed their atmo-suits, Nana left to get the loading process started.

Soon the three men were warming their bodies with wonderfully delicious hot chocolate. Jay and Giles sipped theirs from steaming mugs, but John preferred to lap his up out of a bowl.

The loading went very slowly. But the men didn't seem to mind so much because Nana kept pouring out more of the fabulous hot chocolate. Giles drank so much that he seemed to add another few pounds to his big belly.

At one point, Pappy Nana told his guests, "Sorry it's taking so long. It's hard to find good help out here. No one wants to live on Pluto. Seems I'm the only one who likes it!"

After two hours, *Purple Dream* rocketed away from Pluto, filled to the brim with fuel and supplies. Everything was going perfectly for John and his companions. All systems were go for a swift and safe journey to Barnard's Star.

Then the men's luck changed for the worse.

Not far from Pluto, a bright green dot showed on the flight deck's telltale screen. The dot meant another ship was nearby. The bottom of the screen read: LC Z-34.

John turned to Jay, the only other person in the flight deck. "We've got a Legion cruiser on our tail. How did it find us? There is no way anyone could have known we were going to Pluto."

Jay slapped his knee, angry at himself. "Because we were tricked, fooled, suckered! That's why!"

"What do you mean?" John asked, his ears shifting with confusion.

"Pappy Nana was only *pretending* to be our friend," Jay said, closing his eyes with shame. "You see, he must be in on Adam Ulnar's plot to take over the System. While Nana went off to make us hot chocolate, he must have radioed one of Adam's fellow traitors. Then Nana made sure the loading went slowly so the Legion ship would have time to catch up with us. That must be it!"

"We're fast enough to outrun the cruiser," John assured Jay. "If we speed up, there's no way that it can catch us."

A red light began blinking on the telltale screen. The bottom of the screen read: Q-Missile.

"Yes, there is," Jay said seriously. "The Legion cruiser shot a quelton missile at us. And the missile just locked on to our heat source. That means it'll follow us now, no matter how fast we go. That missile will draw closer and closer until . . . we're goners. I guess they're willing to sacrifice Adam. They can still make Eric the Emperor of the Sun."

"Is there nothing we can do?" John asked.

Glancing at a bank of screens, Jay made a quick decision. "There's a nebula nearby. Sal, take us to the Y-C-forty-five coordinate."

"Roger," Sal replied, as the ship veered in a new direction.

"We're going through the nebula?" John asked with alarm.

"Not through it, but near it," Jay explained. "It's our only chance. The fierce heat of the nebula might attract the missile. You just need to cut away from the nebula at the last possible second. It's a risky move, but you're a good pilot, John. One of the best I've seen. Sal, give John manual control."

"Roger," Sal replied.

John shook some nervousness out of his paw, then gripped the joystick. Nebulas were dangerous, John knew. They were areas of wildly swirling gas, so unbelievably hot they could melt the ship and everyone inside it—instantly.

The red light on the telltale screen gave a screeching beep. This signaled that the quelton missile was drawing much too close for comfort. The missile, of course, would also melt the ship—instantly.

Soon John saw the nebula coming into view. It was the most mysteriously beautiful thing he had ever seen. Clouds of gas twirled and tumbled, shaping themselves into fascinating patterns. The gases glowed with intense rainbow colors. It was similar to watching fireworks explode over and over in slow motion.

Near the nebula's center was a blindingly bright circle of reddish-orange. This was a star being born, gradually gathering dust and gas to its core. But it would take millions of years before the birth was completed. It always amazed John to think that stars were mostly just spinning balls of violently hot gas.

Sal spoke in her whispery female voice. "John, you must steer away from the nebula. It will destroy the ship in ten seconds."

"Not yet," Jay told John. "Wait till the last possible second. It's our only hope."

The beeping on the telltale screen grew louder. The missile would strike very soon. John's tongue slipped out, panting with suspense.

The nebula sped closer, dazzling John's eyes with color and spectacle. It was like a gorgeous flower, but dripping with deadly poison.

"Destruction in three seconds," Sal warned calmly.

John kept his direction, heading straight for the slowly forming star.

"Destruction in one—"

John made a sharp tilt of the joystick, causing the ship to swing away from the nebula.

Seconds later, the ship jolted up and down, rocked by a distant explosion. The noise would have been painfully loud, John knew, except for the fact that sound couldn't travel in the emptiness of space.

"It worked!" Jay cried with triumph. "The nebula sucked in the missile and caused it to explode!"

John gave his tail a wag of relief. "You know, Jay, I feel like I'm earning my paycheck this week."

"I'm going to examine the rest of the ship," Jay said, climbing out of his seat. "You know where to take us, John."

Jay left the flight deck. In its usual calm voice, Sal said, "John, what is our next destination?"

John couldn't help but chuckle. *In a way, Sal is lucky not having feelings. We just went through a hair-raising experience, and the computer is cool as a cucumber.*

"Go to the Galaxy One Coordinate System," John told the computer. "Our destination is Barnard's Star. And I'm giving you auto-pilot."

"What shall our cruising speed be?"

John bent back his ears. "Sweetheart, it's time to let this baby rip. Max speed!"

"Roger."

Numbers flew by on the speed meter. John heard a low hum as the ship shifted from its nuclear engine to its geodyne engine.

Through the view shield, John watched the distant stars turn to whizzing streaks of whiteness. John gasped, knowing *Purple Dream* was now increasing toward the speed of light.

Suddenly the stars vanished. Rolling masses of blackness washed over the ship, rather like giant waves of an ocean. The ship was breaking light speed . . . and still going faster.

Finally the speed meter settled at 150 XL.

Oh, I wish my parents could see me now, John thought, feeling his heart pound with excitement. *Their boy is traveling one hundred fifty times the speed of light!*

John Ulnar knew well what an amazing feat that

was. Man had managed to fly faster than the speed of sound way back in 1947. But the speed of sound—around seven hundred miles per hour—was nothing compared to the speed of light, which was 186,000 miles per second! It would be another *thousand years* before man broke the light barrier.

Indeed, many scientists had long believed such a feat was impossible. In the twentieth century, the great physicist Albert Einstein had created the Special Theory of Relativity. That theory stated that nothing made of solid matter could possibly travel beyond the speed of light. Until very recently, that theory had proved true.

The breakthrough came in 2998, when an unknown substance called pymel was discovered in the surface of Pluto. Tiny amounts of pymel contained enormous power and could do almost impossible things. Pymel fuel and the newly invented geodyne engine made faster-than-light travel a reality.

Finally, it was possible for humans to travel the vast distances to the stars. The year 3000 marked the first such expedition. That was when Eric Ulnar led *Purple Dream* and two similar ships to stars outside Earth's Solar System.

Well, back in the present, traveling faster than the speed of light is still a great unknown. It may or may not be possible. But NASA has got some people working on it at the Marshall Space Flight Center, where we'll go in a chapter coming up soon.

The faster-than-light speeds were achieved through a process called "warping." This meant that the ship bent areas of space into a curve. This allowed the ship to cover more "ground" while actually going less physical distance.

John watched the waves of blackness roll by, as if some force were shoveling them out of the way.

I like to think of it as digging through space. Maybe that's because I'm so good at digging. Hey, I wonder if I'll find any bones floating out there!

Wishbone's Time Line of Space Exploration

Here's a history lesson that takes a look back at the *future*.

1957—The first Earth creature is sent into space by Russia. The creature is a dog named Laika!

1969—Two United States astronauts (Neil Armstrong and Edwin "Buzz" Aldrin, Jr.) are the first humans to set foot on Luna, Earth's moon.

2026—An international team of space explorers are the first humans to set foot on Mars. Soon after, other teams land on Venus and Mercury.

2202—Due to overpopulation on Earth, the long process of terra-forming begins on Luna and Mars. Within one hundred years, sizable groups of humans are living on these two bodies.

2376—New technology allows space vehicles to travel at much greater speeds than previously possible. This allows humans to reach the outer planets of their Solar System, or System. This includes Jupiter, Saturn, Uranus, Neptune, and Pluto.

2503—World War III breaks out among the five major Earth nations. Four years later, the war ends with all nations weakened and no clear winner. For more than one hundred years, there are no major advances in space exploration.

2618—The War of Control begins. Five years later, Alexander Ulnar seizes control of all System governments and founds the Purple Empire, a monarchy. Soon after, the empire establishes small colonies throughout the System.

2810—The Great Revolution begins. Two years later, the revolutionaries overthrow the Purple Empire and found the Green Government, a democracy. Soon after, the Legion of Space is founded, and major colonies are established throughout the System.

2998—Pymel fuel and the geodyne engine allow space vehicles to travel faster than the speed of light.

3000—Eric Ulnar leads a Legion of Space expedition to planets in two foreign solar systems.

CHAPTER THIRTEEN

*P*urple Dream zoomed onward, digging and digging through the endless depths of space.

It would take two weeks to reach the Medusas' planet, and there wasn't a lot to do along the way. There was no traffic on the route and no view, except the rolling waves of blackness. Sal maintained the *Purple Dream's* course and speed, needing no assistance from John.

Jay Kalam, the African, spent long hours playing Go with Sal. Go was an ancient Chinese board game, far more complex than chess. The board was set up on the dining table of the main cabin. Jay moved his shiny white beads with his hands, while Sal moved its shiny black beads with magnetic force.

John often watched the game while he did his daily digging exercises. He marveled at how Sal could fly the ship, play Go, and do a hundred other things without ever breaking into a pant.

Giles Habibula, the potbellied Englishman, spent most of his time keeping watch over the engine room. It was located in the rear of the ship's lower level.

The geodyne engine stood in the center of the room, protected by a duro-glass dome. A large ball of shiny-silver metal hovered a few feet off the ground, spinning rapidly. Around the ball hovered a metal wheel that could tilt in any direction. The geodyne engine gave off a steady low-pitched humming noise that John's sharp ears could hear in every part of the ship.

John liked to visit Giles in the engine room because the Englishman usually had some snacks in his pocket.

On one of these occasions, Giles gave a wheezy chuckle as he pulled out a drumstick of roasted turkey. "What do you think of this, lad?"

"Aha!" John said, lifting onto his hind legs. "I thought I smelled something delicious in here."

Giles tore off half of the drumstick's meat for John, and kept the rest for himself. The two men gobbled their portions at practically light-speed.

"You know," John said, licking the grease off his paws, "I'm growing rather fond of you, Giles."

Samdu Samdi, the giant man from Titan, spent a lot of time alone in the cannon room. It was located at the front of the ship's lower level. It was smaller than the engine room, filled with controls for the ship's four cannons and two missile launchers.

Samdu spent hours sitting on the floor in a curious cross-legged position. He was practicing yoga, a form of relaxation that he had learned from his grandfather, who grew up in India.

Sometimes John joined Samdu in the cannon room, where he practiced his own form of relaxation— gnawing on one of his rubber chew toys.

Adam Ulnar, the white-bearded Supreme Commander, spent almost all of his time as a prisoner in his bedroom. A lock had been put on the outside of the door so Adam could not escape. It was feared Adam might try to send a message to his fellow traitors or do something else of a sneaky nature.

The crew's bedrooms were located in the middle part of the lower level. Because the crew was small on this journey, each man was allowed his own room. Jay had generously given Adam the Supreme Commander's cabin, which was larger and more luxurious than the others. A politeness had developed between Adam and the men, everyone knowing they depended upon one another for survival.

One day, John paid Adam a visit and found the man typing away at a computer.

"What are you doing?" John asked Adam.

"I am writing my memoirs, the story of my life," Adam explained. "I'm calling it *The Destiny of Birth*. It should be a fascinating book."

"I'd like to read it when you're through."

Adam fixed his piercing blue eyes on John. "You

might be the only one—unless some publisher on a distant planet finds the document floating in space. You do know, John, that we shall not make it back to the System. The dangers awaiting us are worse than you could possibly imag——"

John turned and left the room, locking the door behind him. Jay had insisted that no man listen when Adam spoke of the dangers ahead. Jay warned that it would only serve to weaken the men's nerves.

As the days dragged on, John Ulnar thought more and more about Aladoree Anthar.

Even though he barely knew the young woman, John's heart ached whenever he thought of her. He pictured her among the colorful flowers of her garden on Mars. He smelled her pleasant scent. He heard her musical voice. He saw her steady gray eyes gazing down at him.

And then he thought of her being tortured by alien creatures on a faraway planet.

Aladoree must be saved. Partly because she alone knows the secret that can save the Green Government from destruction. And partly . . . just because I like her!

On the thirteenth day of the journey, John entered the flight deck. It was time to slow *Purple Dream*'s speed. If the ship was traveling too fast, it would be impossible for Sal to locate the Medusas' planet.

"Okay, Sal," John said, "take the speed down to two hundred thousand XS."

John heard the humming of the geodyne engine fade as the ship shifted back to its nuclear engine. The ship was putting on the brakes, slowing from one hundred fifty times the speed of light to only two hundred thousand times the speed of sound.

Soon the speed meter had shifted from 150 XL to 200,000 XS.

The rolling waves of blackness vanished. Once again, billions of crystal-clear stars glimmered against the background of space. But there was a difference. Now one of the stars hovered very close to the ship, no more than twenty million miles away. Its appearance was similar to that of the sun, except it was much smaller and it burned a bloody shade of red.

John knew this was Barnard's Star.

"Sal," John told the computer, "aim us toward the planet that we have been calling the 'Medusas' planet.' It doesn't even have a proper name yet. You know its location better than I."

"Roger," Sal replied, as the ship shifted into a slightly different direction.

John sat alone in the flight deck, his eyes fixed on the red star.

Why did we never know there were intelligent aliens living so close to us? Only six light-years away. As far as the universe goes, that's practically right next door. Telescopes can't get a good look that far, but still . . . the Medusas must have been very careful not to give away their location. Why? Is there some reason they don't want to be friends with us?

As John watched the blood-red star, his imagination played tricks on his mind. He pictured the star's redness deepening into a strange shade of purple. Then the shape of the star changed into an oval.

As if a wizard had cast an evil spell, it seemed the star was changing into a gigantic purple eye. Just like the eye of a Medusa. And the eye was staring through millions of miles of space, straight at John.

The young pilot felt an icy chill creep through every inch of his fur.

Barnard's Star drifted closer, closer, closer . . .

All right, this story is turning scary. As in *real scary*.

So . . . let's take a break. While John flies closer to his destination in space, let's visit a pretty interesting destination on Earth. Gee, I just love zipping from solar system to solar system!

CHAPTER FOURTEEN

Standing on his hind legs, Wishbone placed his paws against the window of a traveling bus.

That morning, Wishbone and the two academy teams were riding through the spread-out grounds of the Marshall Space Flight Center. Marshall, just a few miles away from the Space & Rocket Center, was the place where much of NASA's cutting-edge technology was developed.

The bus was driven by a big, friendly elderly man who went by the name of Charlie. In addition to driving the bus, Charlie was the tour guide for this field trip.

Charlie spoke into a microphone as he drove. "The first really powerful rockets were built by the Germans during World War Two. They used them as weapons. Well, sir, right after the Germans lost the war, the Russians and Americans wanted to get hold of Germany's rocket scientists and engineers. That was because Russia and the U.S. were eager to beat each other into space. So the Russians took half these men as prisoners of war, and we took the rest."

"I bet they didn't like getting taken like that," someone commented.

"On the contrary, they didn't mind," Charlie said, as he turned the huge steering wheel. "That is because the German scientists and engineers were far more interested in space than they were in war. Besides, the U.S. government treated them very well, and I'm sure the Russians did the same. We brought our prisoners to these very grounds in Huntsville, Alabama. And right here they helped get the U.S. space program off the ground, so to speak."

The scenery was mostly pleasant countryside, with official-looking buildings scattered around. Now and then, however, strange gizmos appeared. Wishbone saw things that looked like giant metal balls sticking out of the ground, and extremely long pipelines that seemed to float through the air. Wishbone figured those devices were used for technology research. The gray, drizzly morning made the sights appear all the more weird.

"The U.S. research was led by a genius of a man named Wernher von Braun," Charlie continued. "He was a big gentleman with a thick German accent who favored fancy clothes. More than anyone else, von Braun was the one responsible for first sending Americans into space. Later in his life, he was also the one who came up with the idea for Space Camp."

David spoke up. "When the government first tested the rockets here, were they afraid everyone watching would get blown up?"

"Von Braun was always very concerned about safety," Charlie replied. "One damp morning, just like this one, von Braun said, 'There is only one danger with testing our new rocket. One of us might catch pneumonia standing outside in this weather.'"

The group had a good laugh at this little insight.

Soon Charlie stopped the bus and took the group into the biggest room Wishbone had ever seen. The windowless, warehouselike space was the size of an entire building. Behind a vast wall of glass, men and women wearing snow-white caps and lab coats were moving around like a hard-working army of ants. They were laboring over a gleaming silver cylinder the size of a sixteen-wheeler truck.

Charlie told the group that the cylinder was to be part of an international space station scheduled to be placed in space soon. The space station would be a joint effort of the United States, Russia, Japan, Canada, Brazil, and a collection of Western European countries. Each country would have its own modules—a self-contained unit—and all of them would be connected to form a sort of floating city a few hundred miles above Earth.

The space station would be used mostly to conduct scientific experiments. However, in the future it might be used for launching vehicles into the deeper regions of space.

"You know what's nice?" Wishbone told Joe and Sam. "How all these countries are finally learning to work together in space. Don't you agree?"

After Charlie showed the group a few more sights at the Marshall Space Flight Center, he drove them back to the Space & Rocket Center. Everyone climbed off the bus, except David and Wishbone. They lingered so they could have a few last words with Charlie.

"Uh . . . Charlie," David mentioned, "I read some-where that some people at Marshall are working on ways to travel faster than the speed of light. Is that true?"

"That's true," Charlie said with a nod. "But it might be a few centuries or more before that becomes possible—*if* it's possible at all. But that's what Marshall is all about—finding ways to take us faster and farther."

"Well, I'd better catch up with my group," David said. "Oh, but I have one last question. How do you know what Wernher von Braun said that damp day about 'catching pneumonia'?"

A smile crossed Charlie's wrinkled face. "Because I was the fellow von Braun was talking to. For the better part of my life, I worked as an engineer at Marshall. Not *all* of them were Germans. Yes, sir, as a young man, I saw the space program grow from a crazy idea into a reality. I'm retired now, but I still like to do these bus tours."

David shook hands with Charlie, then stepped off the bus.

"Thanks for the tour," Wishbone told Charlie.

Looking down at the dog, Charlie gave a friendly wink.

After Wishbone hopped off the bus, he made a startling realization.

Wait a second, Wishbone thought, as he watched the bus drive away. *I know who's been keeping an eye on me for NASA—Charlie! Sure, it must be him. That's why he winked at me. I'll bet he's been around the whole time, watching my every move. When the week is up, he'll go back to NASA to file a report on my progress. If the results are positive, NASA will go ahead with that astrodog program it's been considering. Well, I'd better make sure the results* are *positive.*

12:00 P.M. After putting the finishing touches on the rockets they had worked on the day before, the Charger team took a lunch break in the cafeteria.

Toward the end of lunchtime, Wishbone listened to an interesting conversation among his three best friends. Also present was Andy, the sixth-grader from South Carolina who wanted to be an astronaut.

Sam stopped a spoonful of yogurt halfway to her mouth. "I know space travel is incredibly interesting. But sometimes I wonder if it's worth all the effort and money. I mean, we have so many important problems here on Earth to solve."

"But we can learn so much in space," David argued. "From a scientific viewpoint, space travel is priceless."

"We can discuss this all day," Joe said after slurping up a strand of spaghetti. "But I think humans will keep going into space, anyway. Why? Well . . . just because it's there."

Andy spoke in his polite Southern accent. "I'll tell you folks this. I believe we'll be sending humans to Mars in, oh, say, about twenty years. And I would very much like to be one of those humans."

Wishbone opened his mouth to express his opinion. But everyone was already getting up to leave. It was time for the team to spend some time planning and designing their own lunar outpost.

3:00 P.M. Monique took over for Susan, and the Charger team gathered on the training floor to try yet another simulator. This one looked far more bizarre to Wishbone than the previous three.

There was a big gray wheel about ten feet in diameter. Inside the wheel was a second wheel, and inside that wheel was a third wheel. Inside the third wheel, there was a metal cage with a cushioned chair.

"This is the multi-axis trainer," Monique told the team. "It's also known as the MAT. What it does is spin a person in three entirely different directions. This is used to prepare astronauts for a situation where their vehicle spins out of control."

Theo, a boy with thick glasses, raised a hand. "Is this simulation device going to cause us severe motion sickness? Or, in simpler terms, will it make us puke our guts out?"

After the laughter faded, Monique said, "No, the MAT shouldn't make anyone sick. You won't get really dizzy because you will never spin in the same direction more than twice. And you won't get really nauseated because your stomach stays basically in the same place."

It still doesn't sound very relaxing, Wishbone thought as he eyed the device.

Joe leaned over to David. "Will you be okay with this?"

"I doubt I'll be any worse off than anyone else," David said quietly. "Heights I don't like. But spinning doesn't bother me so much."

Sam nervously twirled a strand of hair. "But *I'm* not so crazy about spinning. Once I went on this spinning ride at an amusement park and I was . . . well, let's just say I couldn't eat anything for a while. I think your Bravo Mission commander may be about to make a huge fool of herself."

"Who wants to go first?" Monique asked the group.

No one volunteered.

"Then we'll start with the commander of the Bravo Mission," Monique announced. "Sam Kepler, come on down."

After receiving a pat on the back from David, Sam walked slowly over to the MAT. She climbed into the seat inside the metal cage, where Monique strapped her in place.

"You'll be spinning for forty-five seconds," Monique told Sam. "If you feel like you need to stop before the time is up, just give a holler."

Sam nodded, but she looked as if she preferred to stop before she even got started.

Wishbone crouched down, partly covering his eyes with his paws. *I don't know if I can even watch this.*

Monique eased down a long lever. With a mechanical whir, the MAT began moving, sending Sam backward, toppling her head over heels and then heels over head. Next, the machine twirled Sam into a totally different direction.

As Monique eased the lever down farther, the MAT spun faster and faster, the two inner wheels and the metal cage twirling in completely different orbits. The whole thing reminded Wishbone of a science project he had seen that showed the crazy spinning motion of an atom.

Sam was flying wildly this way and that—top over bottom, side to side, and at every angle in between. Wishbone tried to catch a glimpse of her face, but she was whipping around so fast her features were a whirling blur. She didn't scream or make any noise, but Wishbone wasn't sure if that was a good sign or not. He wondered if Sam might have fainted from shock.

Finally, the monstrous machine slowed to a stop.

After being unstrapped, Sam stepped out, looking a little shaken.

"How was it?" several trainees called out.

After a long moment, Sam spoke. "Uhhh . . . it was scary. But . . . it was also a lot of fun. I feel just fine!"

Wishbone gave his tail a few wags, relieved that Sam had passed the test with flying colors.

As Sam took a seat, she whispered in David's ear. "I really tried to let go and relax with it. Maybe that would help you deal with the height when you do your space-walking."

David nodded in reply.

One by one, the other trainees took their turn on the multi-axis trainer. Everyone seemed to have a similar reaction to Sam's—the ride was frightening but also fun.

After all the humans had taken a spin on the MAT, Wishbone knew his time had come. He bent back his ears and trotted over to the three-wheeled device.

Monique crouched down to the dog. "Sorry, Wishbone. I don't think it would be a good idea to put you on this."

Wishbone walked away with drooping ears. *Why doesn't she want to put me on the multi-axis trainer? Maybe it's because I didn't do so well on the five-degree-of-freedom chair yesterday. In a way I'm relieved, but . . . I know Charlie is watching me. I can't see him, but I'm sure he's around here somewhere. More than anything else, I have to prove myself to Charlie these next few days.*

My mission is getting almost as important as John Ulnar's mission. John and his fellow soldiers are about to reach—scary music, please—the planet of the Medusas!

Chapter Fifteen

In the distance, Barnard's Star burned with its blood-red fire.

It was the fourteenth day of *Purple Dream*'s journey. A reddish planet had come into view, only a few million miles away—the Medusas' planet. It revolved around Barnard's Star in much the same way the planets of the System revolved around the sun.

John sat perched in his pilot's chair, kept in place by the ship's artificial gravity system. As John watched the reddish planet through the view shield, he gnawed on one of his chew toys. He was doing his best to keep himself from getting too stressed out.

Soon, Jay called John, Giles, and Samdu to the main cabin for a meeting. Adam was also brought in. The five men sat around the dining table.

"For the length of this trip," Jay told the others, "I have refused to let Adam tell the rest of us about the dangers on the Medusa planet. Such talk would only frighten us. However, now we must hear about these dangers."

"And you'd better tell us the truth," Samdu said, showing one of his big fists.

Adam Ulnar, who was both the Supreme Commander of the Legion of Space and a prisoner, folded his hands on the table. His clothes were rumpled and his snowy-white hair unkempt. The man looked tired, as if he had aged several years in the past two weeks.

"I don't expect us to return from this mission alive," Adam said with sadness. "Therefore, I have nothing to lose by telling the truth. Ask me your questions."

Jay leaned toward Adam. "On Eric's expedition to the Medusa planet last year, only one-third of the soldiers returned alive. Explain this."

Yes, please do, John thought, his tail giving a nervous flick.

After a tired sigh, Adam spoke. "Two-thirds of the soldiers died because of something Eric called 'The Belt of Peril.' "

"Oy," Giles said, running a hand through his red hair. *"What* in the world is the Belt of Peril?"

"Do you know what moats are?" Adam asked the men.

John knew the answer. "In the Dark Ages, castles were often surrounded by canals of water called moats. The moats made it difficult for enemy knights and their horses to attack the castle."

Adam nodded. "Well, the Belt of Peril uses the same idea. It's an invisible energy force that surrounds the planet. It's designed to keep away unwanted visitors."

"What does it do?" asked Samdu, a muscle twitching in his thick neck.

"Eric had three ships on his expedition," Adam

explained. *"Purple Dream,* and two others like it. Eric sent the other two ships ahead, while he stayed behind in *Purple Dream.* When the first two ships hit this Belt of Peril, they . . . disappeared."

"What do you mean by 'disappeared'?" John asked, his tail giving another nervous flick.

Adam gripped his hands together, obviously trying to keep them from trembling. "At first the ships shook a bit. Then they began to fade. Then . . . they simply vanished. Apparently, the energy force destroyed the atoms of the ships and everything inside them. One minute they were there, the next minute they were gone . . . forever."

Jay didn't bat an eye. "How did Eric's ship make it through?"

"After Eric saw the two ships disappear," Adam said, "he suspected there was intelligent life on the planet. Using his radio transmitter, Eric managed to contact the Medusas. He explained that he came in peace and would like to meet them. Surprisingly, the aliens understood his words."

Giles gave an irritated snort. "They must have learned our language by picking up the signals from our tele-screen shows. Ha, I knew the blasted tele-screen wasn't good for us!"

"After receiving Eric's message," Adam continued, "the Medusas switched off the Belt of Peril. This allowed Eric's ship to pass through unharmed."

Jay snapped his fingers. "Then we can do the same thing. If the Medusas let Eric through, they may let us through. We shall radio the Medusas. Adam will simply explain that he is an ally of Eric's. If called upon, Eric will say this is true. Remember, Eric doesn't know that *we* are with Adam."

"Are there other dangers on the planet?" Samdu asked.

Adam managed a smile. "Yes, many. But first, let's see if we can make it through this terrible Belt of Peril."

"And we'd better get to work on that," Jay said, rising from his seat. "Gentlemen, to your landing positions."

Minutes later, John, Jay, and Adam were seated in the flight deck. Giles was in the engine room, and Samdu was in the cannon room.

From his pilot chair, John watched the Medusa planet coming closer. It was a big planet, perhaps fifty times the size of Earth. John could now see that the planet was red because its surface was covered with a layer of reddish gas.

"That red gas was put in the atmosphere by the Medusas," Adam told John and Jay. "Barnard's Star is dying. Gradually it shrinks in size, sending off less and less heat. The Medusas have released the gas into the air to keep the planet from growing too cold."

"Is the gas harmful to humans?" John asked.

"Eric and his team found they could survive on the planet without their atmo-suits," Adam replied. "And none of the team suffered any illness after leaving. But they were on the planet for only about eighty hours. For a longer stay, I would suggest the use of atmo-suits, at least part of the time."

When the ship was only six hundred thousand miles away from the planet, Jay nodded at Adam. It was time to attempt communication with the Medusas.

"This will be tricky," Adam warned. "Though the Medusas seem to understand languages from our System, they do not have the ability to speak them. In other words, they may understand *me*, but we will not be able to understand *them*. Also, Eric tells me they have very unusual voices."

John raised his ears. "Then we'll listen closely and try to guess what they say."

Adam turned his chair to face a panel with several com-screens. He fiddled with a control, searching for the proper radio-wave channel. Then he switched on the microphone.

"Ahoy! I am Adam Ulnar, Supreme Commander of the Legion of Space from the Solar System of the humans. I am broadcasting from *Purple Dream*, the ship approaching your planet. Can you hear me?"

A moment passed.

Then a reply came. The com-screen remained blank. But an eerie squeaky-screechy noise sounded through the speaker.

John wiggled his ears with discomfort. "I guess that means 'yes.'"

Adam continued his message. "I am coming to assist Captain Eric Ulnar. He is my nephew, my brother's son. I, too, will be helping you get iron from the Solar System of the humans. Do you understand?"

Again the squeaky-screechy noise sounded.

"I guess that's another 'yes,'" John remarked.

Adam continued. "I am requesting that you turn off the defensive force around your planet. I repeat. I am requesting that you *turn off* the defensive energy force around your planet. Will you agree to this?"

Again the annoying noise came.

Jay turned to John. "Was that a 'yes'?"

"I certainly hope so," John said with a shrug of his paws.

Adam turned off the microphone. "Sal, please activate the PT shield."

"Roger," the computer replied in its whispery female voice.

"What's the PT shield?" John asked.

"It is something I had installed after Eric's trip to this planet," Adam explained. "The PT shield surrounds the ship with protective rays. My hope was to guard the ship against things like the Belt of Peril. However, since my engineers didn't know what the belt was made of, we don't know how well the PT shield will actually work."

"We'll soon find out," John said, taking the joystick in his paw. "Sal, you'd better give me manual control. And strap us in, please."

"Roger," Sal replied, causing the straps to criss-cross all three men in the flight deck.

John bent back his ears, watching the reddish planet draw closer. Soon the ship passed by a brown-ish moon.

Without warning, some kind of force zapped the ship. *Purple Dream* went shaking, jolting, bouncing. The nuclear engine coughed and whined as if it had caught a bad case of the flu.

"Heaven help us," Adam gasped. "They haven't turned off the Belt of Peril. We are going through it!"

"Keep your cool, kid," Jay told John. "The sooner you get us through this, the better our chances of survival."

John saw that the controls were going hay-wire—dials spinning, lights flashing, screens turning to static.

"Ista bakanu jaryblonk," Sal said, its voice program obviously malfunctioning.

John kept a steady paw on the joystick. He ignored the broken controls, using nothing but his pilot's instinct to keep as steady a course as he could. Luckily, after about a minute of rough flight, the ship returned to its normal state.

"Bravo!" Adam cried with relief. "It seems the PT shield fought off most of the belt's power. We are still alive!"

"Nice work, kid," Jay said, reaching over to scratch John between the ears.

Sal's voice returned to normal. "Pilot, I have a damage report. The Belt of Peril has disabled sixty-four percent of the ship's rocket power."

That isn't good news, John thought with great concern. *In fact, it's lousy news!*

The worried face of Giles appeared on a comscreen. "Sal is right. That belt really did a number on the rockets. And there's nothing I can do to fix them while we're in flight."

"That means the ship will crash," Adam said, rubbing his beard thoughtfully. "There is no way we can survive. Except . . . this planet has a very large ocean. If we land in the water, we may have a fighting chance."

"Okay, let's do it," Jay advised.

Sal aimed *Purple Dream* toward the ocean, then turned the ship around so its tail end would hit the water first. This move put all the passengers flat on their backs. A roar sounded as Sal fired the remaining rocket power.

"Get ready for a rough landing," John said, tucking in his tail.

The ship gathered speed as the force of the planet's gravity sucked it downward. John felt himself being

pushed deeply into his seat. The growing pressure of gravity made it seem as if John weighed many times his normal weight.

"Uggghh!" John grunted, as the pressure peeled his black lips away from his teeth.

The reddish gas swallowed the ship, filling the view shield with a swirling redness. The pressure on John grew heavier . . . heavier . . . heavier . . . The young pilot felt as if he might burst at the seams any second!

A shattering noise blasted John's ears. Water rushed past the view shield, millions and millions of gallons of it. *Purple Dream* was plunging through the ocean as if it had been fired from a cannon.

With a violent thud, the ship hit the ocean floor. John gritted his teeth upon impact. If it weren't for the ocean, John knew, he and his companions would have been crushed to death instantly. The ship jerked forward, bouncing into a horizontal position.

Then it was over.

Purple Dream lay completely still. It was stuck on the bottom of an ocean somewhere on a planet in a faraway solar system.

The seat-straps opened. Though his tail was a bit sore, John realized he was still in one furred piece. He looked over to see that Jay and Adam were also alive and well.

"Sal, are you all right?" John asked quietly.

The computer replied, "I am all right, John."

Moments later, Giles and Samdu entered the cockpit. Both of them were also in fine condition.

"Oh, that was *some* landing," Giles said, rubbing his backside. "We pounded that floor like a kangaroo coming down after jumping over a moon. But I'm not complaining. We're lucky to have survived at all!"

"We're not *that* lucky," Adam said gloomily. "Without full rocket power, there is no way to get this ship out of the ocean."

"We'll cross that water bridge when we come to it," Jay said with faint smile. "For now, let's see about rescuing Aladoree. Sal, do you know how deep we are?"

"Approximately sixty feet deep," Sal replied.

Through the view shield, John saw only a darkened blur of ocean. Fortunately, *Purple Dream* was water-tight.

"We're not too deep at all," said Samdu, rubbing at the back of his bald head. "That means we must be very near land. We can make it in the raft."

Jay rose from his seat. "Gentlemen, let us prepare to abandon ship. Adam, are you coming?"

"I would prefer not to meet these Medusas," Adam said with a haunted look in his eyes. "No, I shall remain with the ship. Perhaps I will finish my memoirs."

Everyone went to work. John, Giles, and Samdu went about storing atmo-suits and other necessary equipment in a supply bag. Meanwhile, Jay got Adam to tell him everything he knew about the Medusa planet. He even had Adam draw a map, based on descriptions from Eric.

The preparations done, John, Jay, Giles, and Samdu went to the ship's lower hatch. This hatch had a special entry area that would prevent water from rushing inside the ship. John would be the one responsible for the supply bag.

The hatch was opened. One by one, the men slipped into the waiting ocean.

CHAPTER SIXTEEN

John felt the ocean's water rushing around his fur. As planned, John held onto one of Samdu's pants legs with his mouth. Samdu held onto Giles's legs. Giles held onto Jay's legs. Then Jay pulled a tab on a square device. The device began rising through the water as it filled quickly with air. It was an inflatable life raft, designed for just such a situation.

The ballooning raft lifted the human chain of men effortlessly upward. Soon Jay, Giles, Samdu, and John burst through the water's surface. After gulping in air, the four men climbed into the bright orange life raft, which was now filled with air and ready to float.

After setting down his supply bag, John gave an energetic shake to rid himself of some of the wetness. Then he took a good look at his surroundings.

The sky was covered with a foggy reddish gas that tinted the whole atmosphere red. Almost straight overhead, the blood-red shape of Barnard's Star could be seen burning through the gassy layer. As far as the eye could see, the raft was surrounded by ocean. It looked much like the oceans of Earth, except for the fact that it was an oily shade of yellow.

"Aye, lads," Giles announced, "we're definitely not in merry old England . . . or any other place that looks familiar to me."

When Samdu pressed a button, the raft began to cruise through the water, powered by a small but effective engine. Jay began studying the map of the planet that Adam had drawn.

John settled in for a long raft ride. *So far, things aren't looking so bad. The temperature is pleasantly warm, and the gravity is only a tiny bit heavier than the gravity of Earth. . . . Wait! did I hear something?*

Raising his ears, John turned his muzzle. He saw something pop out of the water a good distance away. It was a smallish froglike head with two antennae that moved easily up and down. It seemed harmless enough.

"Look at that," Samdu said with a smile. "I think it might be some kind of baby creature. It's rather cute, is it not?"

Like a rocket, the creature's head shot into the air. The head was followed by a narrow neck that seemed to be stretching like a rubber band. After covering a great distance, the head and incredibly long neck began curving down toward the raft.

"Maybe it's not so cute after all!" Samdu cried with surprise. "Someone hand me a proton gun. I'll blow the thing to—"

The froglike head was already inside the raft. A long, sharply pointed tongue flicked out of the creature's mouth and seized the supply bag.

"Oh, no, you don't!" John yelped, reaching for the bag with two paws.

But he was too late. As fast as it came, the creature's froglike head zoomed backward. Within seconds, the creature and the supply bag had disappeared underwater.

"I'm going after it!" Giles said, preparing to jump overboard. "All of our supplies are in that bag!"

"No!" Jay said, grabbing hold of Giles.

"That no-good sea creature stole everything!" Giles shouted, his face turning as red as his hair and bushy moustache. "Including all our food and drink! I'm going after it! I'm not letting any demon of a sea creature—no matter how cute or cuddly—take *my food and drink!*"

"I order you to stay put!" Jay said firmly.

Giles was too good a soldier to disobey an order. He sat back down, looking as if he were about to weep.

Feeling water around his paws, John looked

down to see that a hole had been ripped in the bottom of the raft. "I hate to be the bearer of more bad news," John mentioned, "but we've sprung a big leak. That creature's sharp tongue must have done it."

Samdu stared grimly at the hole. "I do not like this planet."

In less than a minute, the raft had sunk. The four men were treading water, adrift in the vast yellow ocean.

John tried to act cheerful. "Listen, fellas, it's not all that bad. Sure, we're six light-years away from home without any food, drink, map, weapons, computers, atmo-suits, or anything else. But look at the bright side—at least the scenery is interesting."

No one laughed.

"We've still got our minds," Jay said, studying the reddish sky. "That should be enough to get us through. Let's see . . . Judging by the position of the star and the course of the wind, we should find land by swimming in this direction. Gentlemen, follow me."

Jay began swimming through the water with easy strokes. Samdu moved along with his powerful arms. Giles huffed and puffed after his friends. John did his dog-paddle.

After three hours of swimming, the men washed up on a flat beach of grainy black sand. Despite the long swim, the men were still in fairly good shape. From here, all they could see was beach in one direction, ocean in the other.

"Luckily, I spent some time studying our map before it sank," Jay told the men. "I have a rough idea of where we should be going."

"Where?" John asked, after shaking off some water. "Medusaville?"

"In a sense, yes," Jay replied. "This planet consists of one giant ocean and one giant land mass, which we are now on. After we travel through a jungle, over a mountain range, and down a river, we should arrive at the planet's only city. That is where all the Medusas live. And that is where we should find Aladoree."

"I wonder if we'll be seeing any other creepy critters," Giles grumbled.

"The Medusas are the only highly intelligent creatures on this planet," Jay explained. "Just like the humans in our Solar System. But Adam tells me there are many plant and animal forms here. And some of them could be quite dangerous. In other words, stay alert."

"We should take some of these," Samdu said, holding up a little silvery seashell. "The edges are as sharp as razors."

Each of the men picked up a shell, which they stored in their pockets. Having nothing more than the shells and their Legion jumpsuits, the men began walking across the beach.

"Oh, I just love vacations," John joked, as his paws pattered across the black sand.

After several miles, the men entered a thick, dark, untamed tangle of a jungle. Bizarre plant forms grew everywhere, creating a strange and bewildering labyrinth. Most of the stems, stalks, and trunks consisted of a ropelike gray substance. Most of the leaves were a shiny shade of blue that looked almost like metal. Scattered about were fuzzy, flowerlike things in a variety of bright colors.

"Owww!" John said, as his tail bumped against a shrub with spiked thorns.

Jay went to examine a treelike growth, dripping

with stringy vines. He touched a peachlike pink thing that grew on one of the vines. "It looks like a fruit of some sort. I wonder if it's okay to eat. Why don't I—"

Just as Jay pulled at the fruit, he was snatched violently off his feet. John whipped his muzzle upward. Jay was high in the air, a vine wrapped around his body so many times the man was helpless to move.

"It's got me tight!" Jay yelled. "I can . . . *uchhh* . . . barely . . . breathe!"

The vine lifted Jay higher, aiming him toward a round orange blossom near the top of the growth. The blossom grew larger, and then it opened into a dark hole with fanglike teeth. Jay's head was headed straight for the mouth. The plant was going to eat Jay alive!

Jay screamed frantically. "Help! Help! Help!"

As Jay kept screaming, Samdu slashed into the base of the stem with his sharp shell. Seeing this, John and Giles took out their shells and began doing the same thing.

A syrupy substance oozed out. The vine didn't let go of Jay, but at least it stopped pulling him closer to its mouth. As John worked with his shell, his ears rang with Jay's helpless screams.

Then John became aware of an awful choking sound. He glanced up, fearing it was Jay. But he discovered that the sound was actually coming from the fanged mouth of the orange blossom.

Samdu, Giles, and John continued slashing at the stem, and soon the whole plant crashed to the ground like a felled tree. Jay landed in a patch of fuzzy flowers, free at last from the vine's deadly grasp.

Jay was trembling in a way John had never seen him. John ran over to help him up.

Meanwhile, Giles was kicking at the fallen plant. Satisfied it was truly dead, he plucked off one of the pink fruits and cut out a chunk with his shell. After chewing for a long time, he reported, "It's as chewy as chewing gum, but you can eat it. It's probably better-tasting than our shoes. I suggest we take a supply."

Jay walked cautiously toward the vined thing. "The plant life here seems to have adapted itself in a very tough and defensive way."

"I've got news for you guys," John said, after biting a thorn out of a paw. "We're getting pretty tough ourselves."

Using their shells, the men set to work on the fallen plant. They cut many pieces of the pink fruit. They also made pouches from the orange blossom in which to carry the fruit. A thick section of the ropelike stem was made into a club, which Samdu took. A long vine was made into a lasso, which Giles took. A shell attached to a long section of the stem formed a sword, which Jay took. A shell attached to a smaller section of the stem formed a knife, which John took.

"Gentlemen," Jay said, waving the men onward, "let us continue."

After about twenty hours of hiking and hacking their way through the jungle, the men came to a mountain range. It looked similar to an Earth mountain range, except every bit of it was formed out of black rock.

At the edge of the range, the men took a brief rest. They wanted to get as far as possible before night fell. Adam had explained that the daylight on this

planet was about five times longer than it would be on Earth. The same would be true of the nights.

John spotted something that looked much like a log of wood from his home planet. Leaning down his muzzle, John began to chew on the log to clean his teeth. With a vicious hiss, the log slithered away from John, quick as lightning.

John's whiskers twitched with surprise.

The men set off across the rocky black range. Sometimes they were able to work their way in between the mountains, but other times they were forced to climb up and over some very high peaks. Aside from the loglike worms, there was no sign of life in the mountains. It was just a wild waste of endless black rock.

"I've never felt quite so much like a mule," Giles muttered as he trudged along.

Soon the men's throats were burning with fierce thirst. John kept his ears lifted, listening for the sounds of moisture. Eventually, his ears led him to a narrow yellow stream that trickled between some boulders.

After lapping some water with his tongue, John said, "It's a bit bitter, but I think it's okay to drink—at least, I hope it is."

Having no choice, all the men drank. Then they filled some of their pouches with the water, sealing them with vines.

On and on, the men trekked across the rough and jagged formations of rock. Each man struggled bravely with his growing weariness. John's four legs ached like crazy, and the rugged ground rubbed at John's paw pads until they were raw. The young officer never once complained, though.

We have to keep going, John thought, as he pushed his paws onward. *We are the only hope for rescuing Aladoree. And Aladoree is the only hope for rescuing the Green Government. I just hate to think of her being held prisoner on this frightening planet.*

After at least thirty hours, the blood-red ball of Barnard's Star was nearing the reddish horizon. The men decided to stop for the night, knowing the planet would soon be too dark and cold for safe travel.

The men entered a rocky cave that would serve as their shelter. They chewed their rubbery fruit and drank the bitter water stored in their pouches. As the shadows of darkness fell, an icy chill crept into the cave.

Samdu had killed a few of the log worms with his club. They weren't edible, but they worked out very nicely as fuel for a campfire. At the academy, the men had learned to make a fire out of practically anything.

John studied his three companions by the fire's flickering glow. Their faces were dirty, bruised, and each had the grizzled beginnings of a beard. Their jumpsuits were ripped and stained. Jay, Giles, and Samdu were starting to look like shaggy animals, and John figured the same was true of himself.

"Och," Giles said, resting his back against a boulder. "This is the roughest tour of duty in my many years as a soldier of the Legion. Compared to this, those battles on the moons of Neptune were a picnic."

"I never knew you fought in the Neptune battles," John said, as he licked at one of his sore paws.

"Aye, lad," Giles said with a wheezy chuckle. "I

suppose that was before you were born. Out there on those moons, I lost half a leg, half an arm, and half an ear. These are replacement parts I'm wearing. Ah, yes, lads, old Giles Habibula has seen quite a bit of action in his time!"

"No doubt this is a tough tour," Jay said after a sip of water. "But I don't believe I will ever serve with a finer group of soldiers."

"And I don't believe we will ever serve with a better commander," Samdu said, giving Jay a proud salute.

On that note of brotherhood, the men lay down to get some much needed sleep. John curled into a furred ball, trying to keep himself as warm as possible. Somewhere far away, he heard a weird whistling howl that set his fur on end.

This is so strange. Here I am, sleeping on a planet with no name in the solar system of an alien star. It makes you wonder. There are billions of stars in the universe, and a lot of those stars might have a bunch of planets revolving around them. There could be trillions of planets out there. How many places in the universe contain living creatures? How many . . . how many . . .

John fell into a deep sleep.

After the length of five nights on Earth, daylight finally arrived on the Medusa planet. The men stepped out of the cave, seeing Barnard's Star burning blood-red through the veil of reddish fog.

Rested and refreshed, the men continued to climb across the black range of mountains. About sixty difficult hours later, the men came to a steep canyon through which a yellow river flowed.

The men killed more of the log worms, which they had discovered could float. Tying the dead log worms together with the vine, the men formed a perfectly seaworthy raft.

The raft carried the men swiftly along the rushing yellow river. John had never been so happy to travel without depending on the use of his paws. After about thirty hours, the canyon walls turned into much lower cliffs.

The men pulled the raft to a riverbank and climbed one of the cliffs. At the top, they saw what they had been searching for. Beyond many miles of black slopes, a city rose eerily from the ground. It was surrounded by a circular black wall that must have reached a mile high. Rising above the wall was a collection of black structures.

John stared at the city, his fur bristling with a mixture of wonder and fearfulness. *It looks like an evil king's castle from some ancient legend. And in that castle, somewhere, waits a captured princess. A princess with a very powerful secret.*

Jay placed his hands on his hips. "Gentlemen, that is our destination. The city of the Medusas. Let us go there at once!"

No, not quite at once. I'm needed back in the present. My fellow trainees at Space Academy and I are due on the training floor for a very important training session.

CHAPTER SEVENTEEN

Wednesday evening, the Charger team assembled on the training floor to practice for their Bravo Mission. Everyone would have a completely different job on the second mission. This time around Wishbone and his three best friends would go into space on the space shuttle.

"Yep, we're going into space," Wishbone whispered eagerly to Joe. "You and me, pal."

The team members were gathered by the vehicle they would be using for their "flight." It looked very much like the space shuttle's *Orbiter,* only it wasn't quite as large as the real thing. The *Orbiter* model was roughly the size and shape of a medium-sized airplane. "Discovery" was painted on the side of the white structure in black letters.

The trainees divided into groups, each of which would be trained for its specific duties by a different counselor. The payload specialists were Wishbone, Joe, and a nice Asian girl named Charlotte. They were taken aside by a counselor named Tina, an upbeat young woman with carrot-colored hair.

After introductions and a friendly pet for Wishbone, Tina got down to business. "Scientific experiments are some of the most important things the astronauts do. And payload specialists are scientists who have been chosen to carry out these experiments. On this mission, you'll be doing actual experiments that real payload specialists do on their missions."

Wishbone noticed that Joe wore a glum expression. *Science is definitely not one of his favorite subjects.*

"The middle part of the actual *Orbiter* is called the cargo bay," Tina explained. "In fact, it's like a big trunk, big enough to carry a bus. Sometimes this trunk carries equipment into space. And sometimes it carries the space lab. By the way, cargo carried into space is known as 'payload.'"

Tina led the group up some steps and into the back of the *Orbiter* model. Wishbone found himself in a rectangular white room. The walls were neatly lined with controls, drawers, and numerous scientific-looking devices.

"This is the space lab," Tina said enthusiastically. "It's pretty much like the lab that the real astronauts use. About fifteen minutes into the mission, you pay-load specialists will leave the flight deck and come in here. I'll show you how to do that a little later. Right now we'll get to the experiments."

"Here we go," Joe muttered under his breath.

"Hang in there," Wishbone urged his pal.

Tina handed one booklet each to Joe and Charlotte. "These manuals describe the experiments you two will perform. Most you'll do separately. Some you'll do together. There are a lot of experiments described in the manuals. You may not have time to finish all of them."

Wishbone raised himself onto his hind legs. "Hey, what about me? I thought I was supposed to be in on this."

Tina scratched Wishbone between the ears. "As we discussed, Wishbone will be part of one of the experiments. It's called the action-reaction experiment. And, Joe, if you think Wishbone isn't enjoying the experiment, we'll stop it immediately."

"I imagine Wishbone will have a great time," Joe said, cracking a smile. "It is me I am worried about."

Tina pointed to a small black chair that rested on top of a yellow cylinder. "For the action-reaction experiment, you will test Wishbone's visual and hearing responses, before and after he does some spinning in this chair. The goal of this experiment is to see how a person's—or, in this case, a dog's—senses hold up after rotational motion."

Wishbone eyed the chair nervously. *Hmm . . . I hope my senses hold up okay. I'm sure Charlie from NASA will be watching this experiment very carefully.*

Wishbone noticed a camera near the ceiling. The camera showed the lab for the benefit of the mission scientist in the control room. However, Wishbone figured Charlie would also be watching.

Tina showed Joe and Charlotte how to operate the chair. Then the three humans and the dog spent some time figuring out a way to test Wishbone's visual and hearing responses.

"We don't actually do any of the experiments until the mission tomorrow," Tina said. "That way we keep the element of surprise."

While Charlotte studied her manual, Tina gave Joe a rundown on some of his experiments. "Let's start with the solar-fluid experiment. You'll find it on page nine of your manual."

Joe leafed through his manual, already looking puzzled.

"In this experiment," Tina explained, "you will expose various fluids to the sun by placing them in a chamber where they would actually be out in space. The goal of this experiment is to learn a little something about solar energy. I know this sounds complicated, but you'll get the hang of it."

Joe nodded, but he looked totally lost.

Tina told Joe to put on goggles and rubber gloves. Then she pulled out a drawer, which contained test tubes filled with colored fluids and a thermometer. Tina began to give Joe instructions about measuring and mixing and working all sorts of mechanical equipment.

Joe looked as if he was getting one of his math-homework headaches. He rubbed his forehead with a gloved hand.

Tina grabbed Joe's hand. "No! Don't ever touch those gloves to your skin. Sometimes they contain traces of harmful fluids. That's why you wear the gloves in the first place."

Wishbone looked at Joe with sympathy. *Poor Joe. He's really struggling with this scientific stuff. I hate to leave the guy, but I'd better go check on David.*

Wishbone stepped out of the space lab, climbed down the steps of the *Orbiter* model, and returned to the training floor.

David and the two other mission specialists were training for their EVA, or space-walk. They were right outside the *Orbiter* model, working alongside a white structure that was shaped something like the letter U. The trainees wore helmets and headsets for safety.

Two trainees were in five-degree-of-freedom chairs, one on either side of the structure. The first was Erica, a girl who had gained a reputation for making goat noises. The second was Nikki, a girl who frequently got a serious case of the giggles. They hung onto the side of the U structure to keep themselves from falling over in their weightlesslike chairs.

At first Wishbone didn't see David. Then the dog looked upward. David was sitting in a manned maneuvering unit chair. It was attached to a long white mechanical arm that worked like the arm of a construction crane. David was suspended over the U structure, a good twelve feet in the air. He looked uncomfortable, as if the boy had just swallowed a handful of live worms.

And I know why, Wishbone thought with concern. *This is the astronaut who's afraid of heights.*

Jenny, the athletic-looking counselor in charge,

spoke into her headset mike. "Okay, folks, let's get to work!"

The three mission specialists were supposed to build a geometrical module by attaching six very long poles together. It would be just like a module that was built by real astronauts in space. The module was called EASE, or Experimental Assembly of Structures.

Jenny gave instructions. Erica pulled one of the long white poles off the U-shaped structure. David sent down a red strap, which Erica attached to one end of the pole. Next, David pulled the end of the pole all the way up to his MMU chair. Then David started to attach a silver prong to his end of the pole, but his fingers were fumbling around too much for him to get it on.

Hmm . . . nobody builds things better than David. But his fear of heights is making him awfully clumsy.

David's partners weren't making the process go any faster. As Erica struggled to hang onto her end of the long pole, which seemed to be quite heavy, she began to make an odd snorting sound. Wishbone recognized this as the girl's famous goat noise. This sent Nikki into a helpless fit of giggling.

"All right, knock it off, you two!" Jenny scolded. "And, David, you need to go higher so you'll have better leverage."

That's the last thing he wants to hear.

Closing his eyes tightly, David pushed a control on the chair. With a whirring noise, the MMU lifted David another foot higher.

Wishbone took a seat on the floor, figuring David could use some emotional support. *That thing may be called EASE, but for David it's anything but EASE. And these trainees will be on a tight schedule*

tomorrow during the real mission. I wonder if they'll even come close to building this contraption.

The session continued to go poorly.

After about forty-five minutes, Wishbone returned to the space lab, where things were going just as badly. Charlotte was doing just fine with her experiments. Joe, however, looked as if he were in the middle of a battle. His hair was a mess and he was surrounded by a clutter of papers, test tubes, and strange scientific instruments.

I'd ask how things have been going, but something tells me I'd better not. I wonder if Joe will be able to complete any of his experiments tomorrow.

"We need to wrap it up in here," Tina told Joe and Charlotte. "Now, let's go to the flight deck. I'll show you the proper way to get from there to the lab."

The group stepped out of the lab, walked past the EVA area, and went to the front of the airplanelike *Orbiter* model. Wishbone, Joe, and Charlotte climbed a few steps and entered the flight deck.

The flight deck was a cramped chamber that looked much like the cockpit of an airplane. Sam, the commander, and Andy, the pilot, were seated up front.

Crouching behind them was Michael, a counselor with wire-rimmed glasses. Sam and Andy were surrounded by gray panels filled with hundreds of buttons, switches, screens, levers, lights, and dials.

Wishbone tilted his head. *Whoa! This flight deck is the most confusing thing I've ever seen!*

In the rear of the flight deck were eight seats, where the rest of the crew would sit during liftoff and landing. Tina took Joe and Charlotte through a hatch at the back of the flight deck, showing them the proper way to enter the space lab. Wishbone decided to hang around and see how Sam was doing.

At the moment, Sam and Andy were working on the part of the mission when they returned to Earth. Andy looked very focused. But Sam looked as if her concentration power was suddenly running low on fuel.

"Okay, now let's work on the RCS maneuver number five," Michael said. "Sam, this is where you will position *Orbiter* at exactly the right angle for its entry back into the Earth's atmosphere. Pilot, you read the checklist, while the commander executes the functions."

Looking at a looseleaf notebook, Andy said, "Find section C-Three, the Orbital DAP. Select System A. Then put the control in manual mode."

Huh? What? Wishbone thought.

Sam studied the complex control panel in front of her. Then she flipped two switches.

Michael leaned forward. "No, Sam, that's not System A."

"Oh, sorry," Sam said, pulling her hands away. "I did it again, darn it. I've been flipping a lot of wrong switches today."

"It's very important that you hit the right ones on the mission," Michael urged.

Yeah, Sam. Don't forget, you'll be carrying very precious cargo on this flight—me!

Sam corrected the problem. Then Andy read through a few more instructions, which Sam followed, pushing buttons and flipping switches.

"Now, turn left for ten seconds," Andy said.

Sam gripped a joystick. As she counted to herself, she pressed the joystick to the side.

"No, you're turning right, not left," Michael said patiently. "That's a serious error. You have to enter Earth's atmosphere at exactly the right time and exactly the right angle. Otherwise, the ship will either burn to shreds or skip off into space forever. That means you have only one chance to get your landing right."

Sam let go of the joystick with frustration. "This is ridiculous! I'm just so concerned about doing things wrong, that I'm not getting *anything* right!"

The counselor put a comforting hand on Sam's shoulder. "Relax. This isn't easy. A real shuttle commander usually has at least twenty years of flying experience before he or she ever takes command of a space shuttle. You get only two hours of practice. Under the circumstances, you're doing just fine."

"Thanks," Sam said with a sigh. "Okay, let's keep going."

Sam continued to struggle with her instructions. Soon Joe, Charlotte, David, Erica, and Nikki were brought into the flight deck by Tina and Jenny, who showed them where to sit. By this point, Wishbone didn't know who looked the most frazzled—Joe, David, or Sam.

"Here you go," Joe said, as he picked up Wishbone and placed him on the seat he would be using. Then Joe pulled a harness across Wishbone's body, strapping the dog firmly into place.

"No, Commander," Michael warned Sam. "That's wrong. Do that, and the shuttle will explode into a mass of fire."

Wishbone shifted uncomfortably on his seat. You know, *I'm having second thoughts about going on tomorrow's mission.*

I'm also having second thoughts about heading back to that terrible planet of the Medusas. But I must be brave for the team. Okay, here I go.

Chapter Eighteen

After traveling many miles along the yellow river, John, Jay, Giles, and Samdu finally came near the city of the Medusas. Then the four men rode their raft along a dammed-off section of the river. This led the men into a giant well made of metal. That seemed to be where the Medusas stored their water supply.

The men managed to climb up the wall of the well. At the top, they stepped onto a ledge that overlooked the Medusa city.

"So this is Medusaville," John said, feeling an uneasiness creep through his fur.

The city stretched as far as the eye could see. It was a very crowded jumble of buildings, towers, domes, platforms, and clumsy-looking machinery. There were no doors or windows in any of the structures, but most of them contained many rectangular openings. By human standards, everything was giant, soaring thousands of feet into the air. And everything was made out of the same boring, blank, black metal.

There were no sidewalks or streets or vehicles or plants, and not a single creature was to be seen. If the men had not known that Medusas lived there, they would have thought they had stumbled upon the remains of a dead civilization.

The city was vast, ugly, and impossible to understand—like something out of a nightmare.

"Nothing like a giant-sized city to make a man feel like a teeny-tiny ant," Giles commented.

The men saw a strange object drifting through the reddish sky. At first, John thought it was some sort of odd flying machine. But, as the object drifted closer, John realized it was *a living thing.*

The creature's body was mostly a big blob shaped like a dome. It was made of a wet, glistening, jellyfishlike substance that was partly see-through and partly a sickly shade of green. Dangling down from the dome were about fifty limply wiggling tentacles. The alien creature looked very similar to a jellyfish, except that its body was as large as an elephant.

When John caught sight of two gigantic purple eyes, one on each side of the dome, he knew what this creature was.

"That's a Medusa," John said, tucking his tail between his legs. "I've never seen a whole one before, but, trust me, that's what this is."

"I see why Eric called them Medusas," Jay remarked. "As I recall, Medusa was a monster in Greek mythology. Instead of hair, snakes grew out of its head. The sight of it was so frightening, it turned men to stone when they looked directly at it."

The creature flew slowly, seeming more like a figure swimming through the sea than one flying through the air. How the alien traveled was a mystery to John, because there were no wings or anything of

a similar nature. When the Medusa was almost over the men, it began lowering.

The men pulled out their crude weapons—the club, the lasso, the sword, and the knife.

At once, four tentacles grabbed the weapons and tossed them away as if they were just toys.

"What do we do now?" Samdu asked nervously.

"I think this Medusa means to capture us," Jay said. "But that may not be so bad. The Medusa may end up leading us to Aladoree."

John felt a slippery, slimy tentacle curl itself around his middle. Three other tentacles seized the other three men. All four men were lifted off their feet, and the Medusa still had several dozen tentacles left to spare.

Keeping a firm grip on the four men, the Medusa floated slowly upward. John's stomach turned somersaults as he saw himself rise to a dizzying height. None of the men spoke, and John figured they were as terrified as he was.

For a long time, the men flew floatingly over the nightmarish black city. The place seemed to go on forever, all of it looking exactly the same. At one point, John saw several other Medusas flying through the foggy red sky.

Finally, the Medusa lowered itself a bit, then drifted through a rectangular opening in one of the gigantic buildings. The Medusa carried the men into an oversized hallway, where another Medusa floated near the high ceiling.

The two Medusas exchanged a screechy-squeaky greeting. Then the Medusa holding the four men pulled down a lever with one of its tentacles.

A circle opened in a wall. The Medusa carried the men through the opening and set them gently on a metal floor. Without a word, or screech, of explanation, the Medusa floated back out through the opening. As if by magic, the circle closed, showing no sign that it had ever existed.

John scratched his side where the slimy tentacle had gripped him. Then he took a look around. He and his companions were in a large, rounded room with a domed ceiling. A dim grayish light lit the room even though there was no sign of a light source. The room was totally empty. It seemed to be a prison cell.

"Well, isn't this just dandy?" Giles said, squinting around at the cell. "Shoved through a hole like a family of mice. And, I dare say, not a piece of cheese in sight!"

Suddenly, John noticed there was one other person in the cell. He was huddled against the wall, watching the newcomers with fearful eyes. The man was a mess. He was unshaven, dirty, and smelly. His clothes were ragged, his longish blond hair greasy and scraggly.

John walked closer to get a better look.

The man scurried away from John like a terrified cat. "No! Please! Leave me alone! Don't do it to me again! Please!"

John realized this pitiful prisoner was Eric Ulnar— the very same Eric Ulnar who had once looked like a movie star, who had achieved fame as a great explorer, who had dreamed of becoming Emperor of the Sun.

"Zounds!" Giles exclaimed. "Look who this is!"

"Please, leave me alone!" Eric cried with fright. "I can't handle it anymore. Not the ji—— . . . the ji—— . . . the ji—— . . ."

Jay hurried over to Eric, grabbing him by the shoulders. "Eric, get hold of yourself! We're not going to hurt you. Do you know who we are?"

"No, I don't," Eric said, his voice trembling and hoarse. "I've been in this dim cell so long, I can't think or see straight anymore!"

Jay spoke soothingly. "You are with Jay Kalam, John Ulnar, Giles Habibula, and Samdu Samdi—officers of the Legion of Space. We have come to rescue Aladoree Anthar, the woman you so unlawfully kidnapped two weeks ago."

"Where is she?" John growled.

"Don't hurt me," Eric said, covering his body in a cowardly manner. "Aladoree is still alive. She's in a cell just down the hallway. And, no, she hasn't yet given away the secret of AKKA."

"Thank goodness for that," Giles said gratefully.

"Why are you locked in this cell?" Samdu asked Eric. "I thought the Medusas were your friends."

"Well, they're not my friends anymore!" Eric screamed like a spoiled brat.

"Get a grip on yourself," Jay ordered Eric. "We need to know what has happened!"

Eric rubbed his face a few times, took a few deep breaths, then spoke much more calmly. "When I first came to this planet, I struck up a deal with the Medusas. I promised to give them iron from our Solar System. In return, they promised to help me overthrow the Green Government. But it turns out the Medusas were lying to me. Who knew those jellyfish even knew how to lie!"

"Why were they lying to you?" John asked.

"They were just using me to get AKKA out of the hands of the Green Government," Eric explained. "They are planning to attack us, and they didn't want the humans to be able to use AKKA against them."

"Why will they attack us?" Jay asked.

"Because their star is dying," Eric said. "They've managed to keep the planet livable for a long time with that red gas. But soon the gas won't be enough, and they will need a new planet. Our sun, on the other hand, is still in great shape. The Medusas have decided they want to seize our Solar System for themselves. All the planets, all the moons—everything."

"Do they mean to share the Solar System with us?" John asked, already fearing the answer.

"No, they don't mean to share it," Eric said in a low whisper. "These Medusas are mean. Meaner than you can imagine. They are simply planning to destroy the human race."

Feeling weak on his paws, John sat down. "When are they planning to do this?"

"Soon," Eric replied. "In a week or so, they will be sending a fleet of ships to our Solar System. Without AKKA, the humans won't be able to fend them off. Of course, the Medusas would also like to learn the secret of AKKA for themselves. That would make things much easier for them. Though their technology is a little more advanced than ours, they still don't have a weapon that can match the power of AKKA."

"But they don't yet have the secret of AKKA," Giles said hopefully. "Isn't that what you told us?"

Eric shook his head. "They have tried very hard to get the secret out of Aladoree. But she won't tell them a thing."

"Brave woman," John whispered under his breath.

"Then they forced me to help," said Eric, turning his eyes away shamefully. "At first I told them I wouldn't do it. But they tortured me until I agreed. Each time I failed to get the secret from Aladoree, the Medusas tortured me some more. They used a thing that I call the 'jiggle-beam.' It's not exactly painful, but it . . . tickles you silly and . . . Oh, it's too horrible to describe!"

The memory of the jiggle-beam was too much for Eric. He crawled over to the wall and began to weep.

John gave himself a thoughtful paw scratch. *It seems the deadly game has changed. This is no longer a battle between the Green Government and the Purple Empire. This is now a war between the Medusas and the human race. And no game has ever been played for higher stakes.*

John walked over to Eric and gave the weeping fellow a few comforting licks. Even though Eric Ulnar had been a low-down, lying, scheming traitor to his government, John couldn't help but feel sorry for him.

Jay spoke as he paced the cell. "Gentlemen, I know our situation looks hopeless. But we must not surrender. We must find a way to overcome these Medusas. The safety of the human race depends upon us. I am ordering everyone to think! Let us use the blessed power of our minds!"

John, Jay, Giles, and Samdu fell silent, each man thinking very hard. Eric continued to weep against the wall.

Finally, a desperate plan was formed. The men discovered there was an opening low in the wall that faced the hallway. It was covered by an air-flow grate. Samdu felt sure he could tear off the grate, after which the men could squeeze through it. After escaping, the men would locate Aladoree's cell and set her free. Then the men would get Aladoree to build AKKA, which she had claimed she could do with very simple materials. This done, the men would order the

Medusas to help them travel back to their Solar System—or else they would destroy the Medusas with the power of AKKA. It would be a convincing threat.

Once all this was worked out, Eric offered a comment. "Fellows, I hate to ruin your fun, but there is always a Medusa standing guard in the hallway. Or perhaps I should say 'floating guard.' How will you get past it?"

Jay thought a moment, then said, "We will just have to fight it face to face—even though I'm not sure the thing *has* a face."

"How?" Samdu asked curiously.

Jay knelt down, giving John a scratch on the back. "Kid, I'm afraid you are going to have to lead the fight against the Medusa out there. Are you up to it?"

John raised his ears to attention. "Yes, I am, sir."

CHAPTER NINETEEN

A few minutes later, John poked his muzzle through the opening in the cell's wall. Samdu had just pulled out the air-flow grate, very silently.

The opening led to the giant-sized hallway right outside the cell. At the other end of the hallway, a Medusa floated near the ceiling. It looked like a giant helium-filled balloon. The Medusa waited at a spot where one hallway turned into another hallway. This was the only way out of the area.

The alien thing was terrifying. Its big, bloblike, greenish, see-through body pulsed in and out, almost in a breathing rhythm. It showed no other sign of movement, except for the slight wiggling of its many tentacles.

Samdu is a lot bigger than I am, John thought nervously. *Why couldn't he have gotten this job? . . . I know, I know—we needed the smallest man for this assignment.*

According to the plan, John would get the Medusa to come attack him. This would accomplish two things. It would keep the Medusa occupied, and it would bring the Medusa as low to the ground as possible. Then Jay, Giles, Samdu, and Eric would attack the Medusa and attempt to kill it.

John slipped his body through the opening. He stood in the hallway, right beside a strange device made of poles, wires, and tubes. The men had seen this device earlier and were planning to use it as a weapon.

Very slowly, the Medusa turned its domed body until one of its two purple eyes focused on John. The mere sight of the eye seemed to fill John's veins with ice.

The young officer froze with fear.

Oh, no . . . oh, no . . . oh, no! At the worst possible moment, I'm so scared I can't move a muscle!

The eye never blinked. It only stared—so big, so liquidlike, such a strange shade of purple. The pupil in the center was as black as outer space.

Why am I so afraid right now? Sure this giant alien jellyfish is nothing to celebrate about. But I've faced plenty of other dangers lately.

Though it was only an eye, it seemed to have all sorts of evil powers. The eye seemed as if it could cast a magical spell over John's body, freezing it. The eye seemed as if it could ease its way into John's mind, searching there for his most secret thoughts. The grotesque purple eye seemed as if it could do *anything* it so desired.

Maybe I'm so afraid of this creature simply because I've been so afraid of being afraid of it. Huh? No, that makes sense. Maybe I'm more afraid of my own fright than I am of the Medusa. In other words, my greatest fear is fear itself!

The Medusa then floated toward John, moving in its slow underwater way. Though the thing was the size of an elephant, it could float through the air with perfect ease.

Okay, I don't have a lot of time, but let's analyze this quick. What is fear? It's something that happens when you sense a threat. It's like an alarm bell ringing inside your body, warning you to watch out. Every living animal feels it—from the most ferocious lion to the tiniest worm. It's a natural and useful response to a dangerous situation. In other words, fear is good. It's nothing to sneeze at.

The Medusa began lowering, slowly, silently. John became aware that the limply wiggling tentacles were coming closer to his frozen body.

And yet . . . there are times when being afraid gets in the way of dealing with the thing that's causing the danger. And I believe this might be one of those times. In other words, John, stop shaking in your boots and do something!

Baring his teeth, John gave the Medusa his most menacing growl. He got the response he had been hoping for.

Fast as a flash, one of the tentacles lashed at John.

"Sorry, you missed," John said, as he darted out of the way.

Again the tentacle lashed. Though the Medusa's body moved slowly, the tentacles could react quick as lightning.

"Nope, missed again," John said, making a nifty move.

Furiously, the tentacle lashed again.

John rolled across the floor, escaping the tentacle. "As they say in the game of laser-ball—three strikes and you are out!"

John knew he was making the Medusa mad, but that was part of the plan. He was hoping to keep the

Medusa from noticing what Jay, Giles, Samdu, and Eric were about to do.

John raced to the end of the hallway opposite his cell. The Medusa floated after John, its tentacles now whipping about like so many angry snakes. Through the swirling mass of tentacles, John saw Jay, Giles, Samdu, and Eric slip out through the opening in the wall.

John lifted onto his hind legs, calling out to the Medusa, "Oh, I get it. You want to dance. Say, what do you guys call this step? The Medusa mambo?"

A tentacle seized one of John's front paws, squeezing it tightly. John sank his sharp teeth into the slimy thing. The tentacle pulled away.

"Yeah," John snarled, "that'll teach you to keep your—"

Several tentacles at once coiled around John's furred body. John was flipped sideways, then yanked roughly into the air.

"Hey, listen, I was just having some fun with you," John said in his best smart-aleck voice. "No need for any hard feelings. Did anyone ever tell you that you have beautiful eyes?"

Then the Medusa began rising with John still in its grasp. But suddenly it stopped. As planned, the Medusa had been too busy with John to see Jay, Giles, and Eric sneaking up on it. By then, each of the three men had a firm grip on a tentacle, with which they were managing to keep the alien creature in place.

The Medusa released an ear-bending screech.

Samdu ran over, carrying a long pole with a spiked point that he had pulled off the unknown Medusa device. Using the pole like a spear, Samdu jabbed the pole into the Medusa's bloblike body. The

Medusa jerked away, but Jay, Giles, and Eric prevented it from floating to safety.

Again and again, Samdu drove his pole into the Medusa's jellylike form. Each time the Medusa thrashed, causing the tentacles and John to go twisting wildly about.

"I'm hurting it," Samdu called out. "But I don't seem to be killing it or drawing anything like blood."

"And I don't know how much longer we can keep our grip on these tentacles!" Giles yelled. *"Owww!* One of those things just got me good!"

"Try an eye," Jay advised Samdu.

"I'll try," Samdu called back. "But I don't if——"

Still caught in the tentacles, John noticed a golden light bursting forth from a bulb on the Medusa's underbelly.

Suddenly, John felt currents of electricity or something like it oozing through his body. From the tip of his tail on up, John felt a ticklish-quivery-shivery-jiggly sensation. His whiskers, tail, ears, and every fur on his body went twitching out of control.

"Aaaaaahhhh!" Eric screamed, crumpling helplessly to the floor. "The jiggle-beam!!!"

John could see that the other four men were suffering the same awful sensation that he was. Even so, Jay and Giles managed to keep their grip on the tentacles.

As the golden glow dimmed, the jiggle-beam eased off. But John felt certain the jiggle-beam would strike again.

"Samdu!" John cried out. "There's a kind of bulb-like thing on the underbelly. I think it's causing the jiggle-beam. It might also be the heart or something equally important! See if you—"

A tentacle snapped around John's muzzle, shutting him up. Obviously, the Medusa did not like what John was saying.

"What was that?" Samdu yelled as he lifted the pole, attempting to jab the alien's purple eye.

Unable to speak, John got a brilliant idea. He began to grunt out a message in the Legion's tapping code. Over and over he grunted: *Round thing on belly. Stab it. Round thing on belly. Stab it.*

Seeming to understand, Samdu fought his way through the wiggling sea of tentacles, batting them back with his pole.

The golden glow burst forth, sending the awful jiggle-beam shooting through John's nerves.

Twitching from the jiggle-beam, the mighty Samdu jabbed the pole straight into the glowing golden bulb. The Medusa jerked away with such violence that the tentacles released John, flinging him clear across the hallway. As he had learned at the academy, John rolled to soften the fall.

With a loud squishy thud, the Medusa fell to the floor. The creature was injured but not dead. The tentacles kept flailing around with what seemed to be a mixture of pain and rage. The jiggle-beam had stopped, and John could see that the golden glow had once again dimmed.

Thunder boomed outside, followed by the sound of rain hammering against the metal side of the building.

Samdu, Jay, and Giles rushed to the fallen Medusa. As Jay and Giles pulled back the wiggling tentacles, Samdu stabbed the creature in the dim golden bulb.

Staggering to his four paws, John realized his friends would soon kill the wounded Medusa. *I don't like killing, but this is necessary. After all, these creatures are planning to destroy the entire human race. They are evil. Or, at the very least, they're not very nice.*

John ran down the hallway until he saw a lever on the wall, similar to the one the Medusa had used to open his cell. John pulled down the lever with his mouth. As if by magic, a circle opened up in the wall. John leaped through it, finding himself in another round and dimly lit gray cell.

Aladoree, the Keeper of AKKA, lay peacefully asleep on the metal floor.

The young woman looked paler and thinner than when John had last seen her, and her glorious gold-red-brown hair had lost some of its glow. But, to John, the lady was still a vision of heartbreaking loveliness.

John lowered his muzzle and gave Aladoree a gentle lick on the cheek.

Aladoree's eyes opened—gray, steady, and honest, as John remembered them.

John spoke in his most manly manner. "It is I, John Ulnar. Officer of the Legion of Space. I have traveled trillions of miles through space to rescue you."

Aladoree sprang to her feet, staring at John with disgust. "It's you! The traitor! Get out of here at once!"

It was hardly the reaction John had hoped for.

John tried again. "Aladoree, I wish to save you. Please, you must trust me!"

"I will trust no one whose name is Ulnar," Aladoree said coldly. "I remember how you locked up those three guards on Mars so Eric could kidnap me!"

"Look, I made a mistake with those guards, but—"

Jay stepped through the circular opening. "Aladoree, you must come with us at once."

"You, I trust," Aladoree said very nicely.

Jay led Aladoree out of the cell. John followed, his ears drooping as they had never drooped before.

John saw the Medusa lying sprawled in the hallway, a lifeless blob. The eyes were still wide open, but now they seemed completely harmless. As John stared at the dead creature, he heard the sounds of a violent rainstorm outside. Giles and Samdu each gave Aladoree a hug, which the young woman warmly returned.

This is just swell. She's thrilled to see everyone but me! Is it my breath?

Giles showed Aladoree the strange device with the poles, tubes, and wires. "Can you make AKKA by using only these items? Is there any chance?"

"I believe I can," Aladoree said, running her eyes over the materials. "But I will need some time to work."

"Where is Eric?" Jay said.

Everyone looked around. There was no sign of Eric Ulnar in the hallway.

"I'll tell you where Eric is," Aladoree said bitterly. "He went to inform the Medusas of our escape. No doubt he hopes they will treat him well for tattling on us. He is a coward."

"I fear you are right," Jay said. "That means we don't have much time before the Medusas come after us. Where can we go?"

"Follow me," Aladoree urged.

She led the group down the windowless, giant-sized hallway. They turned into another hallway, where there was a rectangular opening high on the wall. Each helping the other, the five people managed to climb through the opening.

They entered a rounded room. The only thing in

the room was a big, round tub made of black metal. Samdu lifted John so he could peer into the object. The tub was totally empty except for a circular drain in the floor.

"What is it?" Samdu said.

"Well," John replied, "I think it's either where the Medusas drink or bathe or go to the bathroom. But there's a very large drain on the bottom. Perhaps the drain leads to some type of sewer system through which we can escape."

Each helping the other, the five people climbed into the tub. They managed to pry the drain cover loose. Fortunately, the opening was big enough even for Samdu to fit through.

John stuck his muzzle into the opening. "I hear water down there, but it sounds pretty wild. The rain-storm must be causing an overflow. It doesn't smell so nice, either. The four of us are trained for this sort of thing, but I'm worried about Aladoree."

"You need not worry about me," Aladoree said, pushing John aside. "I can survive just fine!"

Aladoree lowered herself feet first into the drain, then let go. John heard her fall through the air, then hit the water. John took a breath, then jumped through the hole.

Paws pedaling against empty air, John was falling through a pitch-dark pipe. John tilted himself backward and tucked in his tail, knowing that any moment . . .

With a shattering splash, John's hindquarters hit the water, followed by the rest of his body. John fought his way to the surface, but there was no time to catch a decent breath.

He was carried swiftly through a horizontal pipe,

the water rushing along like the wildest of rivers. John heard someone fighting the water ahead of him, and he realized it was Aladoree. Soon John heard voices behind him, which he knew belonged to Jay, Giles, and Samdu.

Giles yelled through the darkness, "Oh, ho, this is very nice! We're swimming through the sewers like a pack of brainless rats!"

Hearing a desperate gasping noise, John realized Aladoree was in trouble. He doubled the power of his dog-paddling, forcing himself to move faster ahead.

Soon he caught up with Aladoree. She was struggling to keep her head above water as the current carried her roughly along.

John grabbed part of Aladoree's garment in his

mouth and hauled the lady's head safely above the water's furiously foaming surface. John kept a hold on Aladoree as the two rushed together through the sewer pipe.

Soon Aladoree yelled over the water's angry roar, "I'm better now! You can let go!" She took a few deep breaths and continued. "But, thank you, John! You saved my life! I am sorry for not trusting you! I see now that you are a brave soldier and an honest man!"

John felt his heart soar upward. If he hadn't been so busy dog-paddling, he would have wagged his tail with happiness.

Thank goodness we're out of that awful Medusa pound . . . I mean prison. But John and his buddies must still find a way to save the human race.

Come to think of it, my Oakdale friends and I still have some important duties to attend to. Let's zip on back to Space Academy.

Chapter Twenty

Thursday arrived, the day of the Bravo Mission.

For the morning's first activity, however, the two trainee teams hiked to a small lake at the edge of the Space & Rocket Center's grounds. Wearing bathing suits, the two teams did some water exercises that required the use of teamwork. Then the two teams were pitted against each other in a raft race.

Each team had a military life raft. One team member would ride in the front of the raft, paddling with his or her hands, while another team member would hang off the back of the raft, kicking with his or her feet. The rafts would go to the center of the lake, circle a counselor, go back to shore, and then two new team members would take over, relay-style. Wishbone rode inside his team's raft as a cheerleader.

As the race came to its last lap, the other team had a slight lead over the Charger team. But then Joe took the front position of his team's raft.

His arms plenty strong from his many hours of basketball workouts, Joe pulled his team's raft through the water with powerful, evenly paced strokes.

"Go, go, go, go!" Wishbone barked as his raft sailed speedily through the water.

As Joe seemed to find even more strength, the Charger team's raft edged into a lead, then hit the finish line first. The entire Charger team burst into big cheer.

"Way to go, team!" Joe shouted, pumping his dripping arms high in the air.

11:00 A.M. After changing out of their bathing suits, all of the Charger team members gathered on the ground floor of the Habitat. It was time for Sam to show the finished version of the team's patch.

Sam pulled out a piece of paper from a folder and held the paper against her chest. "Well, I haven't had tons of time to work on this, so no promises here. But . . ."

Sam turned the paper around. Everyone moved in closer for a better look.

The patch was spectacular. A border ran around the circular patch, showing the last name of every team member. The area inside the border showed stars twinkling brightly against a black background. The stars were so nicely drawn that they actually seemed to glow.

The center of the patch showed a dog's head in profile. The ears were held high, the eyes alert as those of a bald eagle. The dog looked quite a bit like Wishbone.

No one said a word for a few moments. Then everyone spoke at once, marveling at how Sam had created something so inspirational with only a pack of colored pencils.

Wishbone threw his voice into the mix. "I have to

say, that is one handsome dog. Let me ask you, Sam, did you have anyone special in mind when you drew him?"

"I'm glad you guys like it," Sam said, blushing even as her hazel eyes beamed.

1:00 P.M. After lunch, both academy teams gathered in a grassy field that served as a launch site. The rockets the trainees had built were placed on a launch stand, a long metal strip that could hold sixteen rockets at a time. Electrical fuses ran to a "firing box" a safe distance back from the rockets.

The trainees from both teams waited behind a wall with shatterproof windows. Joe held Wishbone up so his pal could watch the action.

A counselor in charge of the launching stood by the firing box. He turned to the group and called, "Who's got rocket number one?"

A boy named Christopher ran over to the counselor. He always had a mischievous glint in his eyes that reminded Wishbone of a mad scientist.

The counselor pushed a button.

Ppffewww! The two-foot rocket shot upward with a sizzling hiss. In less than a second, the rocket was sailing high overhead, leaving a trail of white smoke. The second stage shot away from the first stage, propelling the rocket even higher. Soon a parachute popped out, and the rocket's second stage floated gently to the ground.

With a sly smile, Christopher turned to the group. "I put a cricket in that clear-plastic compartment. I'm sure it made it back to Earth just fine."

Wishbone turned to Joe. "That kid is going to hear

from a lot of angry cricket protestors. And when those crickets get angry, they make a lot of noise."

Most of the rockets flew fairly well. Others didn't. Two fizzled on the pad, two made crazy zigzags, one exploded in midair, and one shot backward, causing the group behind the wall to scatter. Sam's rocket flew a nice course, but the parachute didn't open. Joe's shot up ten feet, changed its mind, then took a nose-dive into the ground, after which the parachute popped out.

"I'm glad I didn't put a cricket in there," Joe remarked.

David's rocket soared the highest and farthest and completed its mission with a perfect parachute landing.

"Space travel," David said proudly. "It seems like magic, but it's really just a bunch of well-placed nuts and bolts. Or, in this case, glue and cardboard."

2:30 P.M. Both academy teams gathered in the auditorium. Each team made a presentation of the lunar outpost that they had designed the previous day. Then the two teams competed in a Space Bowl Quiz, hosted by a panel of counselors. Unfortunately, the Charger team lost the Space Bowl to the other team.

Wishbone felt pretty sure this was because none of his team members listened to his answers.

5:00 P.M. At dinner in the cafeteria, Wishbone parked himself on the floor right near Joe, Sam, and David. The entire Charger team was wearing light blue Space Camp jumpsuits, which they had bought that afternoon in the museum gift shop. It was their way of getting psyched up for the evening's Bravo Mission.

After finishing his dinner, Wishbone noticed his friends weren't eating with their usual gusto.

Sam twirled a fork in her spiced rice. "I'm concerned about the Bravo Mission tonight. I do not think I am prepared."

"Welcome to the club," David said, putting down his knife. "Yesterday I was so nervous up there on that MMU, I could barely breathe."

Joe held up his hands for attention. "Oh, you two should have seen me in the space lab. I was getting so mixed up with all those scientific facts and figures, I wanted to crawl inside a test tube."

"I probably shouldn't tell you this," Sam said, after wiping her mouth with a napkin. "But your brave Commander Sam destroyed the *Discovery* almost every time she pressed a button."

The confessions broke the tension a bit, and the three kids shared a good laugh.

"Well, this should be a challenge for us," David said, after a last mouthful of applesauce. "Today we all did great at things we are good at. Tonight we will have to test ourselves at things we are not so good at."

"So we're a little nervous," Sam said with a simple shrug. "Last night, we spent some time studying our scripts and manuals. We've prepared for these challenges as best we can. Right?"

Joe stood and picked up his tray. "In our rocketry lesson the other day, we learned about Isaac Newton's Third Law—'For every action, there is an equal and opposite reaction.' Maybe we need to make a slight adjustment to that. For every bit of fear we feel, we need an equal and opposite amount of courage."

Wishbone was glad to see his friends looking a little more relaxed about the mission. Even so, he noticed a scent of nervousness was growing stronger.

Sniffing his fur, the dog realized the nervousness was coming off of himself.

Okay, we're counting down toward the Bravo Mission. Meanwhile, let's check the status of our friends back on the Medusa planet.

CHAPTER TWENTY-ONE

Four men and one woman lay on a black beach bordering a yellow ocean underneath a red sky. They were exhausted.

Finally, John Ulnar rose to his four feet and shook off some water. It seemed like days ago that he, Jay, Giles, Samdu, and Aladoree had been swept through a sewer system, spat into a river, flushed into the ocean, and carried to this beach. But John knew all this had happened in only the past hour.

"I feel like a washed-up fish," Giles groaned.

"Make that a whale," Samdu said, giving Giles a pat on his big belly.

Jay got up and began to arrange a series of poles, wires, and tubes on the black sand. These were pieces stolen from the Medusa device that had been right outside the prison cell. Jay, Giles, and Samdu had clung to them through the sewer, river, and ocean.

John stared at the objects. *Now everything depends upon Aladoree being able to turn this pile of stuff into AKKA. That's the only way we can force the Medusas to*

*send us back to our Solar System. Well, at least that awful
yellow rainstorm has stopped.*

"Let me work unwatched," Aladoree said, as she
knelt down to the objects. "I should have AKKA built
in less than an hour. Hopefully, the Medusas won't
find us before then."

The four men walked a ways down the beach so
Aladoree could work in peace. The men were too
tired to do anything but rest their tired bodies on
the sand.

John lay down, stretching his four paws outward.
He looked at his companions. Their beards and hair
were shaggy, their clothes ragged, their skin scarred,
their bodies thick with grime and foul smells.

*I'm sure I don't look any better. At this point, I probably
look more beast than man.*

John gazed up at the blood-red globe of Barnard's
Star. As the star angled toward the horizon, the gassy
red sky gradually grew darker. Soon the long and cold
night would fall upon the planet.

"In a way, I feel sorry for the Medusas," John
said. "Their sun is dying. In several billion years, our
sun will start dying, too. Then, just like the Medusas,
our ancestors will need to find themselves a new
solar system to live in."

"I sympathize with the problem," Jay said in his
usual cool manner, "but not with their methods. They
could have gone looking for another solar system
besides ours that was livable. Or they could have
asked us to share our Solar System with them."

"Would we have agreed?" Samdu asked. "Perhaps
yes. Perhaps no."

Giles sighed wearily. "I fear that humanity stands
at the edge of a war worse than any other."

John whipped his head around, hearing a swishing sound.

A strange creature swooped down from the sky, landing right beside the four men. It looked something like a dragonfly, except it was as large as a man. A pair of paper-thin wings was attached to a furred body with lobsterlike claws.

John crouched in a defensive position, the fur of his tail bristling.

Totally unafraid, Samdu walked right over to the creature. "Listen, whatever you are, I'm in no mood for games today. Either leave us alone or—"

The creature's mouth opened, sending out a fierce jet of flame.

Dodging the flame, Samdu threw one of his muscular arms around the creature's head. He gave a quick twist. The creature reached for Samdu with one of its claws, then sagged lifelessly to the ground.

Giles walked over to the dead creature, scratching his head thoughtfully. "It looks like a dragonfly, but I think it was more dragon than fly. I wonder if we can eat this thing."

The men were so starved that they decided to give it a try. Jay found a sharp silvery shell on the beach and used it to cut into the creature's furred body. He sliced out chunks of meat and passed them around.

John went to work on his portion without delay. Aside from the fact that the meat was raw, gooey, and smelled like a chemistry experiment, it wasn't all that bad. As he ate, John looked over at the mangled creature that had provided his meal. He couldn't help but admire how beautiful the wings were. They were colored a jeweled blue, with traces of pink and gold running through them.

Soon Aladoree approached. "Care for a bite of strange alien insect?" John asked her. "It tastes better than it looks."

"No, thanks," Aladoree said. "I just wanted to tell you that AKKA is almost built. But I've discovered none of those pieces contains any iron. Iron is necessary for AKKA. I just need a piece about the size of a nail."

"Oh, no," Jay said, his piece of meat slipping from his hands. "Legion soldiers never carry anything made of iron because it interferes with the magnetism of our ships. The Legion ships have no iron on them either."

"Indeed," Samdu said, after wiping some goo off his face, "there is not a speck of iron in this solar system."

John felt his tail go limp. He realized that with no iron, there would be no AKKA. And with no AKKA, there would be no way to get back to the System or to fend off the Medusas. And that meant all of humanity was doomed.

With tears filling his eyes, Giles said, "I am reminded of that old child's poem. How does it go? 'For want of a nail, the shoe was lost.' Something like that."

For a long time, the five weary, dirty, defeated humans sat silently on the black sand. It was one of those times when it seemed there was absolutely nothing else to be done.

Then a miracle happened.

John sprang to his feet as he saw a black spidery vehicle in flight over the ocean. It looked just like the Medusa ship that had kidnapped Aladoree from Mars. Attached to the bottom of the ship was *Purple Dream.*

"Look!" John cried, pointing a paw. "The Medusas must have figured out our ship was on the bottom of the ocean. Perhaps we can somehow get to the ship, fix the rockets, and fly home?"

"I wonder what happened to Adam Ulnar," Giles said with a snort. "Either he's dead, or he's going to meet those Medusas after all."

Jay watched the path of the two ships. "I believe they are carrying *Purple Dream* to their city. Even if we could make it back to that city, we probably couldn't make it to wherever they will be storing the ship."

Samdu shook his head hopelessly. "There's no way to get anywhere in that town without a pair of wings."

John looked at the gorgeous wings of the dead creature. "An instructor at the academy once told me I was such a good pilot I could probably fly anything. Maybe now is the time to find out if that's true."

"Lad, what are you talking about?" Giles asked.

"The wings!" John shouted.

It was a wild idea, but it was the only hope. The four men and Aladoree set to work, using the wings and some of the leftover materials from AKKA. The wings were attached to poles that tied with wire to John's front paws. When darkness fell, the group worked by firelight. Finally, after many hours of trial and error, the strange device was actually flyable.

In fact, the wings worked beautifully. Strategy was discussed. Then it was time to set off in search of *Purple Dream*. As a good gust of wind blew by, John trotted along the beach . . . and the wind lifted him gracefully up . . . up . . . up. . . . John had become a glider-plane, able to soar freely on nothing but currents of air. He could rise, lower, or maneuver turns by making slight adjustments with his body and winged paws.

I can *fly anything!* John thought, giving his tail a triumphant wag. *No, don't wag. That might throw off your balance.*

Soon John was soaring over the ugly black structures of the Medusa city. Almost invisible in the night's darkness, John glided his way to a series of landing platforms. Even in the darkness, John had no trouble picking out the silver shape of *Purple Dream*. Tilting his body forward, adjusting his wings, John swooped down for a perfect landing right beside the ship.

And he found himself face to face with Adam Ulnar, the Supreme Commander of the Legion of Space.

Adam's snowy-white hair was combed, and his beard neatly trimmed. Indeed, the man looked years fresher and younger than when John had last seen

him, on the bottom of the ocean. Adam was alone, with no Medusas around.

Adam smiled at the sight of the strange wings. "You are quite a pilot, John."

John didn't smile back. "I am taking *Purple Dream*. Do not try to stop me."

"I'm on your side now," Adam stated.

"I don't believe you," John snarled.

"I knew *Purple Dream* was our only hope of getting back to the System," Adam said, crouching down to John. "So I radioed the Medusas and told them I would assist them if they would raise my ship. They did so, but they also locked me up. However, I managed to escape and make my way up here. Only moments ago, Sal and I finished repairing the damaged rocket systems. *Purple Dream* is ready to fly."

John eyed the Supreme Commander suspiciously. "Now I suppose you plan to return to the System and carry on with your wicked plan to overthrow the Green Government."

"No," Adam said, looking John straight in the eye. "Down on the bottom of that sea, I did some serious thinking. I remembered the heroic actions of you, Giles, Jay, and Samdu, and how you four ordinary men were willing to die for your government. I doubted that you would have been willing to die for an Emperor of the Sun. I came to realize that this was because a free democracy, like the Green Government, is *right*."

John nodded, believing Adam was speaking honestly. "Well, if we don't get back to the System soon, there won't be any Green Government. There won't even be a human race."

"What do you mean?" Adam asked.

John explained to Adam how the Medusas were planning to destroy all of mankind.

"All of this came about because of my selfish dream," Adam said with quiet shame. "Perhaps now I can undo some of the damage I've done. I wish there was time to find Eric, but there isn't. Come, John, let us go save our Solar System!"

John gave Adam a friendly nudge with his muzzle. "King Arthur, welcome back to the Round Table! Now, could you help me get these wings off?"

Minutes later, John climbed into *Purple Dream*'s pilot seat, and Adam sat beside him. Adam and Sal had done an excellent job repairing the ship's rockets, and John blasted away from the Medusa city. Soon John landed on the beach where his friends were waiting. Jay, Giles, Samdu, and Aladoree climbed aboard and the ship blasted off again.

John, Jay, Adam, and Aladoree sat in the flight deck. Giles went to the engine room, Samdu to the cannon room.

Purple Dream soared through the reddish layer of gas and burst into the black freedom of space.

"We'll be hitting the Belt of Peril soon," John said, guiding the ship with the joystick. "Sal, you'd better turn on that PT shield."

After a pause, Sal spoke. "It seems the PT shield has been removed from the ship."

John's ears jumped. *"What?* Sal, did you say the PT shield has been removed?"

"That is correct, John," Sal replied.

"Those evil Medusas!" Jay said, slapping his knee. "They must have removed the shield in case we tried to escape in the ship. I'll bet that's why they're not

chasing us. They know we can't make it through the Belt of Peril alive!"

Adam rubbed his beard, thinking. "I have an idea. I believe the belt's energy force comes from the many moons surrounding the planet. However, the moons are the farthest apart right above the planet's north pole. There's a chance the belt will be a bit weaker there. Try it, John. It's our only chance."

John steered the ship in the suggested direction. Seeing one of the planet's brown moons in the distance, John knew the ship would be hitting the Belt of Peril very soon.

John bent back his ears with determination. He knew he was about to have his piloting skill tested as never before.

The brown moon came closer—and the invisible energy force zapped the ship.

"Hang on!" John barked.

As it did the last time, the ship began shaking like a leaf in a gusty wind. All the flight controls went haywire. Sal began speaking in phrases that sounded like Chinese spoken backward.

Then something even stranger happened. A mist of sparkly, rainbow-colored particles filled the flight deck. The particles danced around joyously, as if they were guests at a fun-filled Mexican fiesta. The mist grew thicker by the second, as more and more particles joined the party.

John felt his fur tingle, from the top of his head to the tip of his tail. When John glanced at his paw on the joystick, he saw it was growing fainter. It was fading away like a melting chunk of ice.

Turning to Adam, John saw the same thing was happening to the man's entire body. All of Adam's flesh and all his clothing were turning so faint they were becoming see-through.

The Belt of Peril is working, John thought with panic. *This mist is nibbling away at our atoms, making them disappear. Pretty soon our bodies will vanish into nothingness. I need to do something different. . . . I know—I'll steer a zigzag course. That might help weaken some of those invisible rays.*

John angled the joystick, sending the ship in a new direction.

"Have mercy on us!" Jay exclaimed. "I can see right through my skin! I see tissue, veins, muscles!"

John felt every bit as afraid as he had those times when he had gazed into a staring Medusa eye. But he knew he couldn't become the slave of his fear now. With Sal and all the controls out of whack, everything depended upon the pilot.

John decided there was only one thing left to do—laugh. He would keep himself together, both mentally and physically, by laughing through his fear. As John angled the ship in a new direction, he let loose a loud laugh.

"What is so funny?" Jay asked.

"Oh, I just thought of a joke," John announced. "I'll tell it to you. Did you hear about the passengers who went through the Belt of Peril and noticed their whole left sides were disappearing?"

"John, are you going mad?" Jay said with confusion.

"Did you hear about them?" John asked again, as he shifted the ship in a new direction.

"No, I didn't," Jay replied.

"Well, they're all *right* now!" John said, his laughter growing louder.

The thick mist of rainbow-colored particles skittered about, as if they found the joke hilarious.

"What's wrong with him?" Aladoree asked.

"He's using his laughter to rebel against the terror," Adam explained. "It's all right. He's flying the ship beautifully."

"You bet I am," John said, easing into a chuckle. "Now, let's try another joke. Do any of you know what would happen if the Milky Way froze over?"

"No, we don't," Aladoree said. "Please, tell us."

"It would turn into a zillion buckets of ice cream!" John said, breaking into a new wave of laughter.

John stole a glance at Adam. The man was still fully alive, but now John could see all the way through to the bones of the man's skeleton!

"Here's another," John said, as he angled the joystick yet again. "Does anyone know why the pilot crashed into the nebula?"

"No," Adam replied. "Tell us, John."

John howled with glee. "He wanted to be a star!"

John found this last joke the funniest of all. He laughed and chortled and guffawed . . . and then it seemed that the mist was thinning out . . . and then John thought he saw his paw returning to normal . . . and then he fainted, collapsing in his pilot's seat.

Wow! This is a scary flight. My friends and I at Space Academy are also about to face a challenging flight. It's time for the Bravo Mission, where anything is possible!

Chapter Twenty-Two

It was Thursday evening, and the Bravo Mission was under way.

Wishbone was strapped into his seat on *Discovery*'s flight deck. Near him sat the payload specialists—Joe, Wishbone, and Charlotte—and the mission specialists—David, Erica, and Nikki. They waited silently. The first part of the mission was all in the hands of Sam and Andy, commander and pilot. In addition to wearing their headsets, all the humans wore their recently purchased Space Camp jumpsuits.

Wishbone ran his eyes around the many controls in the dimly lit flight deck. His tail thumped anxiously against his chair.

A screen up front showed the mission time: T–2:24.

Getting close. Only two minutes and twenty-four seconds until liftoff.

Wishbone heard the capcom's voice coming through the headsets. "Commander, the oxygen vents are closed and the vent arm is retracting."

"Roger," Sam said, appearing much more focused than she had during the training session.

215

Several large screens were arranged around the front of the flight deck. They would show the view as seen on a real shuttle mission. At the moment, they showed the view looking down from near the top of the launch pad. From this dizzying height, Wishbone saw the Cape Canaveral shore jutting out into the Atlantic Ocean.

Yikes! It's scary up here. And we're just parked on the floor. The real astronauts wait on their launch pad hundreds of feet in the air, their craft strapped to gigantic rockets that carry thousands of pounds of explosive power. You know something? It takes guts to be an astronaut!

"Commander," the capcom said, "the ET is now at flight pressure."

"Roger," Sam replied.

Wishbone's thoughts turned to the dog Laika—the first Earth creature ever sent into space.

Wishbone imagined a bitterly cold November day. The time, 1957. The place, Siberia—a large region in the northern part of Russia. That historic day, Laika, a determined Russian mutt, sat in a cushioned compartment of a capsule called *Sputnik II*. At the time, people had jokingly called it "Muttnik." The capsule was perched high atop a towering rocket, waiting to be blasted into the unknown blackness of space.

What was going through Laika's mind? All alone at the top of that rocket. Preparing to go where no man or dog had ever gone before. It's impossible to say. But I know this—of all the brave souls who have traveled into space, there have been none braver.

Wishbone's heart skipped a beat. The mission clock showed: –0:11, –0:10, –0:09, –0:08, –0:07 . . .

Wishbone heard and felt a loud rumbling all around him. He was actually vibrating in his seat.

–0:04, –0:03, –0:02, –0:01, 0:00.

Hearing a tremendous boom, Wishbone folded down his ears. The dog was vibrating so much that he would have fallen out of his seat if he hadn't been strapped into it.

Then the dog realized *Discovery* was actually *moving*. It wasn't shooting high into the air like the real shuttle. But it was moving forward on tracks, just enough to give a sense of how a real blastoff might feel.

On the screens, Wishbone saw blue sky streaking by. It was a lot like watching out the window of a moving car, only far more exciting.

I don't care if this isn't the real thing. I feel as if I'm shooting into space!

Wishbone heard the capcom's voice. *"Discovery,* you're nearing Mach One, the speed of sound. Go for throttle down."

"Roger," Sam said, as she pulled down a lever.

Wishbone kept his eyes glued to the screens. A blur of sky and clouds went hurtling by. The view and the motion combined to make Wishbone's stomach twist and turn just as if he were really zooming past the speed of sound.

At T+2:00, Sam ejected the solid rocket boosters. At T+8:45, Andy ejected the external tank.

Then the screens showed only blackness. *Discovery* had entered the dark, silent, mysterious world of space.

Sam fired the OMS engines, which released a sound much like the angry roar of a dragon. This put *Discovery* into its orbit around Earth. On the screens, Wishbone saw the colorful, cloud-covered ball of his home planet, two hundred miles below.

Wishbone leaned forward in his seat. *I told Sparkey, my golden retriever friend, I'd wave to him if I could. But I can't seem to find Oakdale down there.*

It was time for the payload specialists to get to work. Joe unstrapped himself, then Wishbone. At the rear of the flight deck, he stepped through a hatch, followed by Wishbone and Charlotte. If they had really been in space, Wishbone knew, they would be floating rather than walking.

The trio went into an entry chamber. Joe and Charlotte spent a few moments flipping switches that sent power into the space lab. Then Joe pushed a button, a hatch whirred open, and the three payload specialists entered the white-walled laboratory.

Wishbone glanced around at all the controls, drawers, and scientific equipment. Then he looked at the black chair that was perched on a tall yellow cylinder. He knew the experiment involving him and the chair-spinning would be the first.

All of a sudden, fast as a flying comet—the dog was very scared.

Why didn't they put me on that multi-axis trainer yesterday? Wishbone thought, as he scratched his side frantically. *Maybe they thought I couldn't handle it. And if I can't handle that, I may not be able to handle this chair. What if I fail? What if I'm just not cut out for this astrodog profession!*

Wishbone caught sight of the camera near the ceiling. The eye of the camera lens was pointing directly at him.

The dog stopped scratching. *Oh, that's right. Charlie is watching my every move. Calm down. This isn't just about me. This is about following bravely in Laika's pawsteps. And this is about leading the way for all those*

218

other dogs with dreams of being unleashed in space. I can do this. Okay, fellas, put me in the chair!

Joe lifted Wishbone onto the chair and strapped him securely in place. Then Joe walked a short distance away and picked up a device. One hand held a small black box, while the other hand, hidden behind his back, held a control device.

Charlotte watched, a pencil poised to record data on a clipboard.

Joe spoke very clearly. "Wishbone, remember what we practiced yesterday? When you hear a beep or see a light, give a bark. Got it? See beep or hear light. Bark."

"Yes, I remember," Wishbone said, placing his senses on high alert. "We practiced it over and over in the training session."

With the hand behind his back, Joe hit a button. A beep came from the box. Wishbone barked.

Seconds later, a red light appeared on the box. Wishbone barked again.

Charlotte recorded the response times on her clipboard.

"How did I do?" Wishbone asked nervously.

Charlotte gave no answer. Instead, she flipped a switch, causing the chair and Wishbone to rotate. The chair didn't spin wildly out of control, but the speed was enough to turn the room into a whirling blur of whiteness. After thirty seconds, the chair stopped.

Wishbone shook his ears to clear his thoughts.

When the box beeped, Wishbone barked. When the box showed a light, Wishbone barked again.

After making some notes, Charlotte spun the chair again. Round and round the white room turned, revolving in a never-ending circle. After sixty seconds, which seemed to last forever, the chair stopped.

Ahhh, this time I feel a bit dizzy. Come on, concentrate. Think of something that will really get you focused. I know— a big, delicious, meaty bone.

The box beeped. Wishbone barked. The box showed a light. Wishbone barked again.

"How did he do?" Joe asked eagerly.

Charlotte was writing on the clipboard. "I'm just impressed that he understood the instructions. But his action-reaction times are excellent. They show very little slowing down after both rotations."

Wishbone glanced up at the camera and gave a wink. *Hear that, Charlie?*

Joe came over and gave Wishbone a good scratch. "Way to go, boy. You've inspired me. If you can do these experiments, then sure as shooting, so can I!"

"That's the spirit!" Wishbone said, giving Joe's face a sloppy lick.

With newfound confidence, Joe put on a headset and punched a button on a panel. "Mission scientist, this is Joe. Charlotte will give you a report on the action-reaction experiment. And I'm about to begin the solar-fluid experiment. Over."

Joe lifted Wishbone down from the chair. The dog made himself comfortable on the floor, his tail wagging with satisfaction over his recent success.

Joe and Charlotte dived into their experiments. Charlotte was doing as well as she had the day before. The surprise was Joe. He was working swiftly but precisely—pouring liquids, taking temperatures, writing notes, punching buttons, operating instruments.

What do you know! Maybe I did *inspire him. I think I'm going to give myself a new job on this mission. MCCB. Mission Courage and Confidence Booster. Hey, I'd better go check on David.*

Joe and Charlotte were so wrapped up in their experiments that they didn't see Wishbone reach up to hit a button with his paw. The hatch to the lab whirred open.

Wishbone went back into the entry chamber. Instead of continuing back into the flight deck, he made a left turn, which took him into a long tunnel lined with blinking lights. At the end of the tunnel, the dog entered a small chamber used by the mission specialists for putting on their spacesuits. Wishbone stepped through a hatch—and he was floating in space.

He was really just on the training floor. But for the purpose of the mission, this was considered space. The mission specialists were already at work, building the EASE module just outside the model of the airplanelike *Orbiter.*

The mission specialists were wearing bulky white spacesuits and big helmets, which made their job even more difficult. Erica and Nikki were dangling in their five-degree-of-freedom chairs, hanging onto the side of the U-shaped structure.

Wishbone forced himself to look up.

The long crane arm was lifting David, sitting in a manned maneuvering unit, high into the air. Wishbone noticed that David was taking deep breaths, his eyes firmly shut. Obviously, the boy was still struggling with his fear of heights.

In his new role as MCCB, Wishbone sounded a courage-and-confidence-boosting bark.

Still rising upward, David opened his eyes. When he spotted Wishbone on the floor, a smile spread across his face.

Well, a smile is a good sign.

David's chair came to a stop about thirteen feet off the floor. Amazingly, all of a sudden David seemed much more comfortable with the height. Eyes wide open, he took a good look at the training floor below, almost as if he were seeing it for the first time.

What do you know! Maybe I inspired David, too!

"Erica, Nikki," David said into his helmet mike, "let's get busy with this thing. Time is short."

Looking very ready for business, David tossed down his red strap to Erica, who attached one of the long white poles to it. Then David hoisted the heavy pole upward.

Wishbone sat down to enjoy the EVA show. Led by David, the three mission specialists worked together beautifully. Erica and Nikki were attaching the bottoms of the poles to the U-shaped structure in various places. David was joining the tips together very expertly with silver prongs.

After a while, the six poles had been formed into a three-dimensional triangle that rose from the U structure.

"Okay, that's it," David told his fellow mission specialists. "We have a perfectly built EASE. Ground crew tells me we still have nine minutes left on our schedule. Plenty of time to enjoy the view!"

Wishbone gave his tail a wag. *David did a fine job up there. He must feel ten feet tall—no, make that higher!*

His work done there, Wishbone trotted over to a big white cylinder that was a model of a space station. After figuring out how to enter the thing, Wishbone paid a brief visit to the three payload specialists inside. They were busy performing scientific experiments.

Not wanting to miss his ride home, the dog said good-bye to the three astronauts. He made his way back inside the *Orbiter* model, trotted through the tunnel with the blinking lights, passed through the entry chamber—and stepped back into the space lab.

"There you are," Joe said, as he jotted down some data. "I was wondering where you went. Here, boy, check this out."

Joe tossed something on the floor, which Wishbone ran over to examine. It was a rubbery ball made of a clear substance.

"That's a polymer," Joe said, sounding very scientific. "It's a compound made by bonding the molecules of two different kinds of liquid—alcohol and sodium silicate."

Wishbone twitched his ears to make sure he was hearing correctly. "Joe, you sound just like a rocket scientist."

Joe glanced at a screen that showed the mission time. "Ah, wait, it's time to check on my vapor growth system."

Joe pushed a few buttons on a wall, then opened a drawer. After putting on his rubber gloves, he pulled out a small object. It was a chunk of crystal that gleamed an emerald green.

"It's gorgeous," Charlotte said, coming in for a closer look.

"A crystal made from mercuric iodide," Joe announced proudly.

Charlotte put on a headset and pushed a button. "Mission scientist, Joe and I have completed all the experiments in our manuals. That's right, *all of them*. We are going to start cleaning up now. Then we will return to the flight deck."

Hmm. . . . Wishbone thought, as he batted the rubbery polymer ball with his front paws. *This makes a pretty good dog toy. Now and then those scientists come up with something really useful. Well, Joe and David have certainly done an excellent job on this mission. Sam seems to be doing great, too. But I'm afraid she's still got some of the toughest stuff ahead of her.*

At T+1:11:00, Wishbone, Joe, and Charlotte joined David, Erica, and Nikki back in the flight deck. Everyone got strapped in, preparing for the journey back to Earth. All this time, Sam and Andy had remained in the flight deck, piloting *Orbiter*.

Wishbone settled in for a comfortable landing. *The only thing we're missing is a flight attendant to bring us some peanuts.*

The dragon roar of the OMS engines sounded a few more times. Looking as focused as she did during the liftoff, Sam flipped some switches and worked the joystick. She was placing *Orbiter* in exactly the right position for reentry.

Moments later, Wishbone saw the blackness of space ease into the dark blueness of Earth's upper atmosphere. *Orbiter* was plunging toward Earth, pulled down by the force of gravity.

Suddenly, Wishbone spotted a red light on the

caution-and-warning screen. The dog was about to give Sam a caution-and-warning bark, but then she spotted the light herself.

"Uh-oh," Sam said, leaning in to read the light's label. "We've got a malfunction. Let's see, it's a problem with the air data system."

"That's bad," Andy said seriously. "The air data system helps calculate the altitude, steering, and speed-brake control. In other words, if we don't get it fixed, we'll crash, big time."

Then I suggest we get it fixed, Wishbone thought. *Pronto!*

Andy flipped through his manual. "We don't have the solution up here. That means we'll have to get it from the ground crew."

Sam spoke into her mike. "Houston, we seem to be having a problem. Our air data system is malfunctioning. We need you to give us the solution."

"Okay, we are going to check for that," the capcom replied. "Give us just a sec——"

The voice disappeared in a sea of static.

"What happened?" Nikki, the giggly girl, cried out with panic.

"We just went into the reentry blackout," Sam answered. "There won't be any communication with ground control for approximately three minutes. We'll just have to wait for the answer."

This isn't good, Wishbone thought, feeling a flutter in his stomach. *Sam was having enough problems landing this thing in the training session. This crisis will turn her into a nervous wreck. Okay, this is a job for the MCCB. Sam, I'm sending a very large supply of courage and confidence right your way. Are you receiving?*

With determination, Sam straightened up in her

chair. Though Wishbone could sense the stress coming from the girl, not a bit of it was visible on the outside.

Wishbone glanced at the screens. Across the blueness of the atmosphere, there appeared a semicircle of wildly dancing bright orange light. Wishbone knew the orange glow was caused by gas particles forming around the ship.

At this point, *Orbiter* was falling at twenty-one times the speed of sound. This intense speed created a friction against *Orbiter* so strong that the heat was building up to more than twenty-five thousand degrees. The heat was what caused the gas particles, as well as the radio blackout. The only thing keeping *Orbiter* from burning into liquid metal was a series of protective ceramic tiles on the ship's underbelly.

"Are we going to crash?" Erica whispered tensely.

"What happens if we crash?" Charlotte asked. "I mean, do we *really* crash?"

"No, we don't really crash," David whispered. "This is just pretend, remember."

"And we need to stay quiet," Joe suggested. "Sam and Andy really need to concentrate these last few minutes."

By then, Nikki was getting close to being hysterical. "I know this is just pretend. But why doesn't it *feel* like pretend? Why does it feel as if we're about to burn up or smash into a mountain—or something just as awful? I don't like this! I don't even like flying in airplanes that much! I want to get out of here!"

Very calmly, Sam turned around to face her crew. "Everyone needs to settle down and be quiet. Andy and I will get us down safely. That is a promise."

The flight deck fell silent.

Way to go, Sam. That's the way a commander commands . . . even though we still might crash.

After a very long three minutes, the capcom's voice drifted through the static. "*Discovery*, are you there?"

"*Discovery* is here," Sam replied immediately.

"We need to do this fix really quick," the capcom told Sam. "Otherwise, we'll get behind on the landing schedule. Here's what you do. Find the air data switch on the F-six panel."

Wishbone held his breath. He knew there was no time to waste fumbling around or hitting the wrong control, as Sam had done the day before. A second's delay could mean fixing the problem too late. And that could mean disaster!

Sam ran her eyes over the complicated control panel. She placed her finger on a switch and said, "Got it."

"Switch it over to NAV," the capcom advised.

With a sure hand, Sam flipped a single switch.

Wishbone was very pleased to see the red light on the caution-and-warning screen disappear. Sam had gotten it perfect the first time.

"Thanks," Sam told the capcom with obvious relief. "I see our little problem has walked away."

"Glad to hear it," the capcom said. "Conditions look fine for landing. Pilot, adjust the brake speed to eighty-one percent."

Andy pulled back a lever, then said, "That's a go."

Wishbone became aware that once again he could hear and feel a rumbling all around him. On the screens, he saw light blue sky and clouds streaking by at high speed. Knowing how dangerous these last few minutes could be, Wishbone found himself holding his breath again.

Sam stayed razor-sharp as she prepared for one of her most difficult assignments. As *Orbiter* fell swiftly toward Earth, Sam had to make a series of S-shaped turns to slow the craft down. Otherwise, *Orbiter* would plunge into a very ugly and deadly crash.

With a light touch on the joystick, Sam eased *Orbiter* this way and that, this way and that. Every move of Sam's hand was as smooth as silk, just the way it needed to be.

Suddenly, Wishbone saw the ocean, green land, then a long concrete runway. Sam pulled back her joystick, pitching *Orbiter*'s nose upward. Andy punched some buttons, sending down the landing gear. Within seconds, *Orbiter* began rushing down the runway.

As Sam brought down *Orbiter*'s nose, Andy pulled back a lever, applying the full power of the brakes. *Orbiter* slowed and slowed and slowed and finally . . . came to an easy stop.

Every one of the eight passengers released a sigh.

The capcom broke in. "*Discovery,* welcome back to planet Earth!"

Everyone unstrapped from his and her seat. After Joe got up, he unstrapped Wishbone. The hatch was opened, and one by one the crew climbed out of *Orbiter*. However, Wishbone remained in his seat a moment, all alone in the flight deck.

The place was very quiet and still, as if nothing in the world had just happened.

I just want to spend a moment remembering Laika. Back in 1957, they knew how to shoot a ship up into space, but they weren't so good at getting it back down. As a result, Laika never made it back to Earth. Like a true hero, she gave her life to further the exploration of new frontiers. She never got all the parades and paw-shakes that she deserved. But I'm sure of this—that dog's courageous spirit continues to live.

Wishbone jumped off his seat and climbed out of *Discovery*.

My crew and I made it back to Earth alive and well. But the *Purple Dream* crew is still trying to get back to Earth—if there still *is* an Earth!

Chapter Twenty-three

John woke up, finding himself under the covers of a bed. Every inch of his furred body ached. John noticed the blurry shape of a man standing over him. Gradually, he realized the man was Adam Ulnar.

"Where am I?" John said with a moan.

Adam gave the young man a fatherly smile. "You are on *Purple Dream.* Eight days ago, you guided us safely through the Belt of Peril. As soon as we made it through the belt, everyone on board passed out, except for me. Sal and I have been flying the ship."

"Why did we pass out?" John asked. "Was it from breathing the red gas for so long without atmo-suits?"

"Yes. However, I have created a medicine that seems to help the condition. I've been giving it to all of you. Jay, Giles, and Samdu also woke up today."

"What about Aladoree?"

Worry entered Adam's eyes. "She is in worse shape. This is because she spent much longer on the Medusa planet. I've done all I can for her, but still she lies in a deep trance. She may live . . . or she may not. All we can do is wait and hope."

John saw the blackness of space outside the porthole. "Are we headed for Earth?"

"Yes, but we need to be prepared for the worst. The Medusas may have already begun their war against the human race. Remember, their ships can teleport from solar system to solar system in a matter of seconds."

"Can we get some information about what's happening in our Solar System?" John asked.

Adam shook his head. "All communication channels are dead. I think this is the work of the Medusas. I only hope we can get back to the System before . . . everything we know is gone."

"So do I," John said, forcing himself to sit up.

After putting on fresh clothing, John went to the ship's main cabin. At the dining table, he had a delicious meal with Adam, Jay, Giles, and Samdu. None of the men had touched much food in several days, and they each ate heartily.

Then John paid a visit to Aladoree's cabin. The young woman lay on a bed with her eyes closed. Her skin was almost as white as John's fur. If it were not for the woman's slow breathing, John would have thought she was dead.

John raised onto his hind legs, placing his front paws on the edge of the bed. For a few moments, he gazed at Aladoree's beautiful but very ill form.

Then he spoke, even though he knew Aladoree would not hear the words. "You must not die, Aladoree. You are the only one who knows the secret of how to build AKKA. And AKKA is our only hope of keeping the Medusas from destroying the human race. And . . . there is another reason you must not die. Because . . . I have fallen in love with you."

Aladoree's eyes fluttered a few times, then opened. She turned her head, fixing her sleepy gray eyes on him.

"What did you say?" she asked softly.

Seeing Aladoree awake, John sent his tail jumping with joy. But John was also a bit embarrassed by the words he had just spoken.

"Uh . . . what did I say? Well . . . I said . . . I was very concerned you wouldn't wake up."

"Well, I'm up," Aladoree said with a faint smile. "Thank you for caring. You are a wonderful man, John. Do we know what is happening back in the System?"

"I'm afraid we don't know."

Six days later, the painful truth was revealed.

Purple Dream landed on planet Earth, in the sun-baked desert of New Mexico. Adam had decided that Green Hall, the capital of the Green Government, should be the first stop.

What John saw made his fur crawl with horror. Green Hall lay in ruins. The once splendid complex of emerald-green buildings was nothing more than a mountain of shattered glass and twisted metal. The surrounding parkland also lay in waste. The grass had been burned to brown stubble, the trees charred into ugly black shapes. The dying light of sunset cast the whole scene in deathly shadows.

John was the only one who left the ship. His job was to find a piece of iron, which would allow Aladoree to finish building AKKA, which she had begun to do on the Medusa planet. As John trotted

over the burned ground, his little black nose was greeted by the smells of doom.

John began to wander around the rubble that
had once been Green Hall. Soon he discovered a man
sitting on a broken chair in front of burnt-up desk. He
was an older man, the efficient office-worker type.
John got the feeling the man was trying to fight off
shock by going about business as usual. There were no
other living persons within eyesight.

"Hello, sir," John said politely. "May I ask who
you are?"

The man rubbed some ash off of his business
outfit. "I am an official of the Green Government.
Assistant to the deputy secretary of the Earth
Environmental Agency."

"I see. Can you tell me what has happened? I just
flew in from . . . very far away."

"Last week," the man said after a heavy breath, "all communication channels throughout the System went dead. No one knew why, and no one could fix them. Then yesterday . . . spiderlike vehicles appeared out of nowhere. All over Earth and Luna. The ships contained intelligent alien creatures. Big floating things that looked like jellyfish. If you haven't seen them, I doubt you would believe me."

"Oh, I believe you. Go on."

"These creatures began launching bombs. Hundreds of them. Strange little devices that sent off blinding rays of red light. Each bomb was about equal in power to our Triple-H bombs. This morning I managed to get a UIN report. It said the losses were . . . very bad."

John knew that UIN stood for Underground Intelligence Network. It was an agency responsible for gathering information during times of disaster.

Feeling dizzy on his paws, John sat down. "How bad were the losses?"

The man cleared his throat. "Reports say that all of Luna's human population has been wiped out . . . and perhaps . . . half of Earth's population."

John blinked hard, then asked, "What about the rest of the System?"

"The UIN says the aliens began their attack with Earth and Luna. After they finish destroying the rest of Earth's population, they plan to move on to the other planets, moons, and space stations in the System. Unfortunately, with no communication or super-fast ships available, there is no way for us to warn anyone in those places."

"Do you know where the alien ships are now located?"

The man nodded. "According to the UIN, all the alien ships are now stationed on Luna. Overnight, it seems the aliens have put up a giant, black-walled fortress there. On Luna, the aliens prepare for the next series of attacks. I'm afraid there is nothing the Legion of Space can do to stop them."

"I wouldn't be so sure of that," John said, rising to his four feet. "Good sir, would you like to come with my friends and me?"

"No, no," the man said, waving a hand. "I have some business to finish in my office. But, thank you."

John continued wandering through the rubble. He couldn't let his mind dwell on the tragic loss of life. He needed to find a single piece of iron so Aladoree could finish building AKKA. Then it could be used to destroy all the monstrous Medusas in the System. The only good news John had received was that all the attacking Medusas were gathered in one place, Luna.

Finally, John found a broken toy that must have belonged to the child of someone who had worked in Green Hall. It was a piece of a model train, a type of vehicle that hadn't existed for more than six hundred years. One good sniff told John the object was made of iron.

John took the toy in his mouth and raced back toward *Purple Dream*. Halfway there, he stopped dead in his tracks.

Out of thin air, as if by magic, a giant black ball with curving legs appeared on the ground. It was one of the spidery Medusa ships!

The Medusas on Luna must have spotted Purple Dream *landing on Earth. So they teleported a ship right here. They've come to finish us off before we finish them off. I wonder how—*

235

Suddenly, John saw Jay, Giles, Samdu, and Aladoree hurrying down *Purple Dream*'s ladder. They began running toward a nearby boulder.

"Get back in the ship!" John yelled to his companions. "You can still escape!"

John's voice was drowned out by the roar of *Purple Dream*'s rockets. With a blast of flame, *Purple Dream* shot forward, still in its horizontal position. Spraying dirt and rocks, the ship went zooming across the ground, straight for the Medusa ship.

John understood what was happening. Adam Ulnar was going to drive *Purple Dream* head-on into the Medusa ship, causing both to explode. Samdu could have fired the proton cannons, but they might not have been enough to destroy the enemy ship.

John darted behind some rubble, then covered his head with his front paws.

A deafening explosion rocked the ground. John peeked through his paws to see that both ships had erupted in a gigantic ball of fire. A mass of black smoke drifted into the air. There could not possibly be any survivors.

Adam Ulnar, Supreme Commander of the Legion of Space, sacrificed his life to destroy that ship. He did it for us. And he did for democracy. Bless him, he has died with honor.

It was dark by the time Aladoree finished building AKKA. She was forced to start from scratch because the first weapon she made had been destroyed along with *Purple Dream*. But she had no trouble building a new weapon from scraps found in the rubble. And this

time she had the necessary piece of iron, taken from the toy train.

John, Jay, Giles, and Samdu stood looking at the finished weapon. A small collection of metal scraps, tubes, and wires rested on a tripod of poles. There did not seem to be any power source, such as a fuel engine or an electric battery. It looked like nothing more than a piece of junk.

So this is AKKA, John thought, tilting his head with confusion. *The most powerful weapon ever known to humanity. Aladoree tells us she can destroy every single Medusa on Luna, while keeping the device right where it is. Amazing!*

John looked up at Luna, which was full that night. On the moon's surface, John could see a small black dot. He figured that must be the black-walled fortress where all the Medusa warriors and their ships had gathered.

Aladoree angled a tube so it aimed straight at the moon. Then her fingers made a few movements on the machinery, reminding John of a musician playing an instrument.

AKKA stood motionless, not moving or shooting or even showing the tiniest spark. However, moments later, a weird greenish fog formed around the moon. After about ten seconds, the fog faded away. By that time, John could see that the black dot of the Medusas had vanished from the moon's surface.

Is that all there is to it? How did it work?

Aladoree turned to her companions, her face showing neither hate nor triumph. "It is finished. Our enemies are no more. My ancestor, Charles Anthar, designed AKKA as a weapon to protect the freedom of mankind. And it has done just that. We must continue to keep its secret, and I hope it never needs to be used again."

"I wonder if more Medusas will come," Samdu said, gazing with awe at the moon.

Jay gave a sigh. "I doubt it. The Medusas on the home planet will learn what has happened. And they will leave us in peace. The five of us have served our government well."

"Now we need to locate some drinking water," Giles said, patting his belly. "We'll be getting thirsty soon. And I don't see any camels passing by that might be willing to share the supply in their humps!"

Jay, Giles, and Samdu went searching through the ruins of Green Hall for some drinkable water. Aladoree began to take apart AKKA. John stood nearby, serving as her watchdog.

Many people have died, John thought, as the cool desert breeze ruffled his fur. *The long list probably includes most of the leaders of the Green Government. And yet many more people continue to live. We will just have to go about the task of rebuilding. I'm sure it can be done, especially with men and women as fine as Jay, Giles, Samdu, and . . . Aladoree.*

As John watched Aladoree, he thought she looked more beautiful than ever. She seemed to be a wonderful combination of a goddess and a hard-working woman.

There is something I would very much like to ask that brave lady. I'm a little afraid, though. No, I believe I will do it anyway.

When Aladoree had disassembled the AKKA completely, she came to sit by John.

"Aladoree," John said after an awkward pause, "I've . . . uh . . . been doing some thinking here.

I know it's not really the best of times . . . but . . . uh . . . I was just wondering if you might consider getting married to me."

Aladoree looked at John with her steady, honest gray eyes. John couldn't tell which way the answer would go.

"John Ulnar," Aladoree said, giving John a scratch on the head, "I don't wish to make such an important decision tonight. But, yes, I will consider getting married to you. Perhaps if I become your wife, then I can count on you to do a better job of guarding me. You let me get away once, you know."

John raised his ears to attention. "If you become my wife, I will never let you out of my sight. You have my word as an officer of the Legion of Space!"

Soon, Jay, Giles, and Samdu arrived with containers of water and armsful of wood scraps. The wood was arranged in a pyramid shape and turned into a blazing fire. Then those five brave people who had just saved the human race sat there, enjoying the fire's warmth and one another's company. They also discussed where their next meal might come from.

As humans had been doing since the long-ago days of the cavemen, John Ulnar gazed up at the mysterious night sky. He allowed his eyes to wander among the many millions of glimmering stars. And he thought, with hope, about the future.

Well, I don't know about you, but this story practically knocked my spots off. Oh, yes, it's been a real humdinger of a tale.

But right now it's time to exit the future for the last time and travel back to the present.

CHAPTER TWENTY-FOUR

At noon on Friday, the final day of Space Academy, the two teams and all the counselors gathered in the auditorium for a graduation ceremony. All too soon, the thrilling six days had come to a close.

The camp director who had spoken on the first day appeared at the podium. "Congratulations to all the trainees," he told the group. "And I extend special congratulations to Wishbone, the first dog to graduate from Space Academy."

Many of the trainees turned to look at Wishbone. "No autographs right now, please," Wishbone told the kids.

"Having Wishbone here this week makes an important point for us," the director continued. "We believe Space Camp is for everyone—youngsters of all ages, as well as adults. We also accommodate trainees who are hearing-impaired and visually impaired, and we welcome trainees from foreign countries. Dr. Wernher von Braun believed everyone should have some access to the excitement of the space program, and we at Space Camp believe the same thing."

After a few more words, the director introduced a guest speaker. He was an average-looking man in his forties. With his thinning hair, trim moustache, and nice gray suit, he could have been any businessman on the street. But he wasn't. He was Buck Slessinger, a genuine NASA astronaut.

"So I understand we have a dog that went through the program this week," Buck Slessinger said with a chuckle. "I think that's great, because we've taken many animals up on shuttle missions for experiments. Let's see . . . we've taken fish, flies, bees, mice, rats, ants, frogs, snails, jellyfish . . . and, oh, a few other creatures. I'd say it's about time we took up another dog."

Wishbone's ears perked up. "Hey, that's great news. Here, Buck, let me give you my phone number. It's—"

When Slessinger kept talking, Wishbone realized that probably wasn't the best time to give out his phone number.

After discussing his life as an astronaut and answering questions, Slessinger wrapped things up. "You have to go through a tough selection process to become an astronaut. But any qualified person is welcome to apply. If you're interested, my advice is to get a good education, with a special emphasis on science or engineering courses. There's no reason why there couldn't be a future astronaut sitting in this room right now. So . . . I hope to see at least one of you up there someday."

Most of the trainees wore a curious look, no doubt wondering if they might be that future astronaut.

The director joined Slessinger at the podium. One by one, the trainees were called up onstage to receive a diploma and a pin with a pair of silver wings.

Wishbone went up with Joe, who accepted Wishbone's diploma and pin for the dog.

When everyone sat back down, the director announced, "Now I'd like to present the Right Stuff Awards. This is an honor presented to one member of each team for showing outstanding personal character." The director glanced at a card. "Okay, the winners are Amber Mulberry and . . . Wishbone."

After almost jumping out of his fur, Wishbone trotted back up onstage. Buck Slessinger placed a silver medal attached to a red-white-and-blue ribbon around the neck of each winner. The whole thing went very nicely with Wishbone's dog tags.

As cameras flashed all around the room, Wishbone heard the wonderful sounds of clapping, laughing, and cheering. For a few shining moments, the dog felt like a very famous television star.

Wishbone faced his public, feeling he ought to say a few words. "I'm not much for speeches, but . . . Well, I accept this award on behalf of Laika, who I feel I've come to know, and on behalf of canines everywhere with a big dream. Thank you. Thank you very much. Yes, thank you."

As the crowd noise faded, Wishbone scanned the auditorium. Way in the back, he saw a shadowy shape against the wall. It was dark back there, so Wishbone couldn't quite tell if it was a person or a fire extinguisher. However, the dog felt fairly certain it was a person—namely, old Charlie.

I guess he'll be heading back to NASA now to make his report on me. I think I've proved my point loud and clear. It's definitely time to start that astrodog program. Right, Charlie?

1:35 P.M. Wishbone stood with Joe, Sam, and David in Rocket Park. Seeing the rockets tower into the sky, Wishbone thought they looked like a band of noble knights in armor.

Wishbone and his friends were waiting to be driven to the airport, where they would catch a flight back to Oakdale. Among their many souvenirs of Space Camp were the addresses and phone numbers of the other trainees on their team. The week's activities had brought the Charger team close together, and they planned to keep in touch with one another.

"This week was even better than I imagined," Joe told his friends.

"I think we all found something inside ourselves we didn't quite know we had," Sam pointed out.

David gazed off at the gigantic *Saturn Five* rocket. "It's amazing what people can do when they put their minds to it."

With a bright smile, Joe knelt down to rub Wishbone's back. "I'm really proud of you, boy. I stuck my neck out, claiming you were the best dog to attend Space Academy. And you proved me right. You did pretty great, pal."

"Thanks, Joe," Wishbone said, enjoying the backrub. "But I don't know if 'pretty great' quite covers it. This whole experience was a bit bigger than any of you realize. I'm not really at liberty to give you guys the full details, but . . . this week I'd say I took a giant leap for all dogkind!"

Whew, I'm exhausted! Saving the human race and going through Space Academy at the same time is quite a mission. But I had a fantastic time, and I think I picked up an important message somewhere out there in the dark depths of the universe. If you've got a big dream, don't let every little fear drag you down. Shoot for those stars. There is truly a place for all of us in the Legion of Space!

About Jack Williamson

In the universe of science fiction, Jack Williamson is a living legend.

Born in 1908, young Jack and his ranching family moved around the southwestern United States. Sometimes the family traveled the old-fashioned way, by covered wagon. But Jack was fascinated by the new forms of technology he saw in the world, things like automobiles, airplanes, and radio.

As a teenager, Williamson became a big fan of magazines that published science fiction stories. The mixture of science, fantasy, and futuristic settings in these tales set Williamson's imagination spinning. By the time he was in college, Williamson was sending his own stories to the magazines. Finally, one of them got published!

The twenty-year-old Williamson launched into a career as a professional writer. Over the next twenty years, he wrote a great number of sci-fi stories for several popular magazines. Filled with wonder and adventure, the tales had such titles as *The Doom from Planet 4* and *Invaders of the Ice World*.

After serving in World War II, Williamson saw that sci-fi magazines were giving way to sci-fi books. In 1947, Williamson revised one of his magazine stories and had it published in book form. This was *The Legion of Space*. Over the next fifty years, Williamson published more than fifty sci-fi books. His most popular book is *The Humanoids*, which features a race of dangerous robots.

In his fifties, Williamson became a college professor

at Eastern New Mexico University. Among other subjects, he taught courses in science fiction, which he believed to be a valuable form of literature. The university now houses the Jack Williamson Science Fiction Library, a large collection of important sci-fi books and documents.

In 1976, Williamson was awarded the Grand Master Nebula—the highest lifetime achievement honor given to an author of science fiction.

Now in his nineties, Williamson is still going strong. During his long life, he has watched the rise of such phenomena as television, computers, CDs, and space travel. Sparked by what he sees, Jack Williamson is still imagining the future and sharing his dreams with his readers.

About *The Legion of Space*

The Legion of Space was written many years before humans first went into space. That's the magic of science fiction!

The story first appeared in 1934 in a magazine called *Astounding Stories of Super-Science*. It came out only a few chapters at a time, encouraging eager readers to keep buying the magazine. *Astounding Stories* was a type of magazine known as a "pulp," because the cheap paper came from wood pulp. In those days, before television and computers, pulps were a popular form of entertainment. The pulps featured flashy covers and exciting stories about detectives, spies, cowboys, monsters, and, of course, space travelers.

In 1947, *The Legion of Space* was published in book form. Over the years, Jack Williamson wrote four other books that starred the Legion of Space characters. These are: *The Cometeers, One Against the Legion, Three from the Legion,* and *The Queen of the Legion.*

The Legion of Space is a type of science fiction story often called a "space opera." Like opera, these tales involve grand and passionate battles between good and evil. Frequently, the fate of planets and galaxies is at stake. The *Star Wars* series is another good example of a space opera.

Often science fiction stories take an idea from the historical past and place it in a futuristic setting. For example, the struggle between democracy and monarchy in *The Legion of Space* is an age-old conflict. Sci-fi stories also might take a subject from the present and imagine where it might lead. For example, AKKA in

The Legion of Space springs from the new types of missiles and bombs that were developed in the first half of the twentieth century.

The Legion of Space also contains some literature history. Jay, Giles, and Samdu were meant to be like the heroic Three Musketeers, and John like the young swordsman who joins them. Giles was also meant to be like Falstaff, a "fat knight" made famous by William Shakespeare.

The Legion of Space is not a well-known book to anyone except sci-fi fans. However, it's a fun-filled treasure that is certainly worth digging up.

About Alexander Steele

Alexander Steele is a writer of books, plays, and screenplays for both juveniles and adults. And sometimes for dogs. *Unleashed in Space* is his first Wishbone Super Adventure. He has written *Moby Dog* and *The Last of the Breed* for the Adventures of Wishbone series. He has also written *Tale of the Missing Mascot*, *Case of the On-Line Alien*, and *Case of the Unsolved Case* for the WISHBONE Mysteries series.

Alexander has written fifteen books for youngsters, covering such subjects as pirate treasure, snow leopards, and radio astronomy. He is now in the process of creating a new series of juvenile books. It's about . . . well, he can't reveal what it's about yet. Among Alexander's plays is the award-winning *One Glorious Afternoon*, which features Shakespeare and his fellow players at London's Globe Theatre.

He was born the same year NASA was founded, so, in a way, he and the U.S. space program grew up together. As a child, he was fascinated by the space program. He has a dim memory of John Glenn orbiting Earth in his *Mercury* capsule, and he remembers the landing of *Apollo 11* on the moon as if it were yesterday. While preparing this book, Alexander spent a week at Space Academy in Huntsville, Alabama. Needless to say, he had the time of his life!

Alexander lives in New York City, which is a long way off from Barnard's Star.

THE WISHBONE™ *UNLEASHED IN SPACE* SWEEPSTAKES

Three lucky winners (at least 9-years-old and in 4th, 5th or 6th grade in the fall of 1999) will have a chance to enjoy an exciting, educational week at SPACE CAMP® in Huntsville, Alabama! Enter today! No purchase necessary.

HOW TO ENTER

1. Print your name, address, birthday, and your favorite WISHBONE adventure of all time on the official entry blank or a 3" by 5" card. Official entry blanks available at participating retailers. Mail to:

WISHBONE™
BIG FEATS! ENTERTAINMENT
ATTN: *UNLEASHED IN SPACE* SWEEPSTAKES
P.O. BOX 1638
YOUNG AMERICA, MN 55594-1638

Limit one entry per person. No mechanically reproduced entries will be accepted. Neither Big Red Chair Books™, Lyrick™ Publishing, Big Feats! Entertainment, Lyrick Studios, their sponsors nor agencies is responsible for lost, late, incomplete, illegible or damaged entries. All entries must be received by June 19, 1999.

GRAND PRIZE

2. Three Grand Prize winners will be selected by random drawing from all eligible entries received by June 19, 1999. Grand prize includes a trip for one person to SPACE CAMP in Huntsville, Alabama. Specifically, round trip air transportation and 6 day/5 night stay, including lodging and meals, at SPACE CAMP (total approximate retail value $1,175). Winners must attend SPACE CAMP during the week of July 25-30, 1999, or the prize will be forfeited in its entirety and awarded to an alternate winner.

DRAWINGS

3. Drawings for the Grand prizes will be conducted on or about July 1, 1999, and will be supervised by a representative of Young America Corporation, whose decision is final in all matters relating to the drawings. Odds of winning are dependent on the total number of eligible entries received. All prizes will be awarded. Winners will be notified by mail. Prizes won by a minor will be awarded in the name of his/her parent or legal guardian. Each winner and/or his/her parents will be required to sign an Affidavit of Eligibility. Winners have five days from prize notification to return the Affidavit, or the prize will be forfeited in its entirety and awarded to an alternate winner.

DETAILS

4. The sweepstakes is open to all United States and Canada residents, excluding residents of Quebec, at least 9-years-old and in 4th, 5th or 6th grade in the fall of 1999. Employees of Big Red Chair Books, Lyrick Publishing, Big Feats! Entertainment, Lyrick Studios, all of their respective retailers, sales representatives, subsidiaries, affiliated companies, licensees, distributors, promotion and advertising agencies and the immediate families of each are not eligible. Sweepstakes is void where prohibited, and is subject to federal, state, territorial, providential and local laws and regulations.

5. By entering, entrants and/or their parents agree that Big Red Chair Books, Lyrick Publishing, Big Feats! Entertainment, Lyrick Studios and their respective affiliates are not liable for any injury, loss or damage that may occur, directly or indirectly, from the acceptance of prizes or participation in the sweepstakes. Prizes cannot be substituted, exchanged, transferred or redeemed for cash.

6. By entering, entrants and/or their parents consent to the use of entrant's name and likeness in any and all advertising and promotional materials relating to this or similar promotions which may be offered by Lyrick Studios and/or its affiliates, except where prohibited. Each winner and/or his/her parents may be required to sign a Liability/Publicity Release. Failure to comply with all rules shall result in the immediate forfeiture of any prize.

7. Any applicable taxes on prizes are the responsibility of the respective winners and/or their parents.

8. Winners and/or their parents will be required to correctly answer a skill testing question as a condition of receiving any prize (Canada only).

9. For a list of prize winners, send your name and address on a 3" by 5" card and mail in an envelope to be received by July 30, 1999, to *Unleashed in Space* Sweepstakes Winners List, P.O. Box 3062, Young America, MN 55558-3062.

Sponsored by Big Feats! Entertainment,
2435 N. Central Expressway, Suite 1600,
Richardson, TX 75080-2734

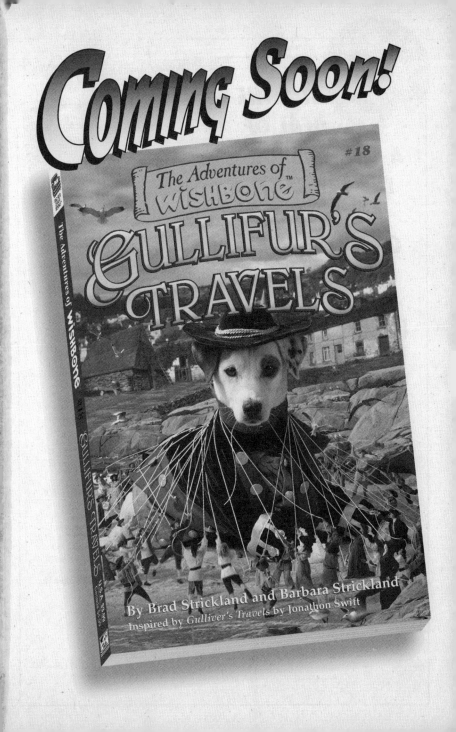